FAKE IT UNTIL YOU MAKE IT SEASON 3

A BIMBO TRANSFORMATION NOVEL

SADIE THATCHER

For all those bimbo lovers out there who continue to support my work. Thank you.

CONTENTS

Introduction   vii

38. The Morning Routine   1
39. Enjoying Life   9
40. Wishlist   17
41. Interrupted Part 1   26
42. Interrupted Part 2   34
43. Helping a Friend   43
44. It Fits   51
45. The Fight   59
46. Making Up   67
47. Do's and Don'ts   74
48. The Fashion Show   82
49. Double Date   90
50. Labels   99

More Fake It Until You Make It   107
About the Author   109
Also by Sadie Thatcher   111

INTRODUCTION

This book is the third "season" of an ongoing serialized story. The story began on my now defunct Patreon and now lives on other serialized platforms. However, the current serialized platform is only available to US readers. For the first time, the broader story of Fake It Until You Make It is available to a worldwide audience in ebook and paperback versions.

Thank you for reading, I hope you enjoy it, and be sure to check out the rest of Fake It Until You Make It story, either in book form when it becomes available, or through a serialized platform.

This season picks up where the previous season left off. The chapter numbers follow the same pattern as the individual episodes in the serialized form. Thus the first chapter or episode in this book begins with chapter 38.

THE MORNING ROUTINE

Jessi woke up Monday morning with a smile on her face. After the weekend she had just had, she was actually looking forward to returning to the more normal school schedule. Or at least the normal school schedule for a hot slut who no longer had to actually worry about her grades. Still, it was the routine that Jessi craved, a semblance of the person she used to be while at the same time embracing her new existence as a sex-obsessed slut.

It started with another shower. This time, however, there was no masturbation or other activity. She was there simply to get cleaned up and ready for her day. After all, she wanted to look her best for Cole. At some point he would view her as ready for him and their real relationship could then commence. At the very least, he could fuck her as she so very much desired.

Jessi had gotten an early enough start with her day to make sure that she was the first to take a shower, since the showers had to be shared among all of the students in the adjacent dorm rooms. The whole section shared the same stalls. At least there was no worry about running out of hot water, but nonetheless, Jessi did not want her morning delayed by having to wait for the other women in the section to finish their own morning routines. Jessi even beat Candi into the showers.

However, by the time Jessi made the return to her room, with only a towel wrapped around her slender and fit body, her fellow students were beginning to emerge from their dorm rooms. A few people smiled at Jessi, but given Jessi's recent behavior, other students scowled at her, obviously not happy to have to live in such proximity to an out and out slut. She had garnered a reputation that made people completely forget about the woman she had been only months before.

"Ugh, some of those girls hate me," Jessi commented as she returned to her room. Candi was up and sitting at her desk, reading her emails on her computer.

Candi looked over at her roommate and watched as Jessi flung off her towel as soon as the door closed behind her. The roommates had no issues with nudity. They needed no modesty around each other. They both had the same goals and worked together to achieve them.

"They're either jealous or they're bitches," Candi explained, as if the answer was obvious. "Some girls are just mean to girls like us, who know how to have a good time and want to look sexy. And others just wish they could be like us. Remember, you used to be one of those girls."

Jessi nodded her head as she looked through her wardrobe, trying to decide what to wear. She was glad for Candi's help. She was also glad that Candi had not outed her as formerly being a boring nerd. Jessi did not know what she would do if she had been rejected by Amy and the other popular girls. It helped that Candi was new to Thatcher

College, although she still had way more experience than Jessi could hope to amass. They were both navigating a different life.

"You're right," Jessi agreed. "I've got to get used to the mean looks though."

"Enjoy them. You've got a good eye for girls with hot slut potential. Amy never would have recruited Elsa. That was all you. You've got more potential than you could possibly imagine. But with those mean looks, you just gotta smile and know you're better than them. They're sad and unhappy and you're hot, sexy, and well-fucked."

"Mmm, yeah," Jessi said as she let a fantasy with Cole take root in her mind. She could only imagine what sex with him would be like, but considering all the sex she had no had in the last week, her ability to imagine had greatly increased. And Jessi had a feeling that Cole had a libido that could match her own. Once they embarked on a sexual relationship, she was certain they would be fucking morning, noon, and night, each and every day.

Candi just shook her head and smirked as she watched Jessi get lost in her fantasy. In some ways, Candi envied Jessi, both for her sudden sexual awakening and for the incredible potential she had. Having already caught the eye of the starting quarterback was a huge achievement. Sure, Cole was still up for grabs, at least as far as sex was concerned, but it was clear that Jessi and Cole had something special brewing. It would just take time to come to fruition.

As Candi returned to checking her email, Jessi shook herself free from the fantasy. She was already wet to start the day, which was not necessarily a bad thing. Jessi bit her lip as she returned her gaze to her wardrobe, looking for the right outfit to wear. Mondays were important to look her best, because she had class with Cole. That was the only important part of her morning now that she had come to her arrangement with Professor Wright. Her classes no longer really mattered, although she still intended to attend them.

Jessi started by pulling out a bra and panty set. The bra was of the pushup variety. Jessi was very aware of her small breasts and always wanted to maximize what she did have. After all, with Candi, Amy, and even Elsa outclassing her in the tits department, she needed to do everything she could to keep up.

The thong that Jessi slid up her legs almost was left alone. If she learned one thing over the weekend, it was that panties were overrated. However, there was something comforting about attending class with a thong on. And it would certainly help her contain her wetness after what would inevitably happen with Cole. He could turn her on like no one else could, leaving her a wet and horny mess. She did not need her juices to leak out of her pussy and either flow down her leg or pool on the seat beneath her.

After that, Jessi's decisions got harder. She needed to find something to wear. She definitely could not go to class just wearing a bra and a thong, even though that would be exceptionally hot. Just the idea of that turned her on even more. Jessi could no longer remember a time when she was not horny. Even her memories of her past life, as being Jessica, were affected by her horniness. She could not imagine herself as being anything but at least a little turned on.

Finally Jessi's outfit for the day started to coalesce in her mind. She started with a skirt. It was a short circle skirt she had picked up while shopping last week. It barely brushed the tops of her thighs and it sat reasonably low on her hips, making it easier to show off her trim midriff. Then again, if it sat any lower, it would reveal the straps of her thong, which was also hot, but a bit trashier than the look she was going for. However, if Cole wanted her to show off her thong while wearing shorts or a skirt, she would do it in a heartbeat.

The top proved the hardest to choose. Jessi glanced out the window and saw that it looked a bit chilly out. It was only the second week of school, but fall was quickly approaching. Jessi was not feeling a jacket yet, so instead she chose a cropped sweater with a deep v-neck that showed off what cleavage her pushup bra could create and nearly the bra itself.

Jessi bit her lip as she looked at her reflection in the mirror. She still needed to apply makeup, but her outfit was complete. She definitely looked good. She looked sexy. And when she added the high heels, everything was perfect. She looked sexy and she actually looked somewhat ready to attend her classes. Not that she was going to be paying any attention to the words that came out of her professors' mouths. Her whole purpose for attending classes was now to spend time with Cole and show off for other male students.

"Join me for breakfast?" Jessi asked once she had finished applying her makeup. Candi did not have a good reason for going out yet, but she was not about to force Jessi to eat breakfast alone.

"Sure," Candi said as she pulled on a tight top that hugged her substantial breasts and made it clear she was not wearing a bra underneath. She already wore a pair of sweatpants with the waistband rolled down as low on her hips as she could get away with.

As the pair walked to the dining hall, it was clear that they were two friends in a slightly different stage of their morning. Jessi was immaculately put together, her outfit, her hair, her makeup, looking perfect. She was ready to go out and tackle the day. Candi looked like she had just rolled out of bed. And the way her blonde hair hung around her shoulders gave her the bedhead look that would make people wonder if she was out late last night getting her brains fucked out. That had not been her night, but she certainly gave off that impression, largely on purpose.

"So what's your plan today?" Candi asked as the pair sat down at a table after getting their food in the dining hall. It was still early, so there were only a handful of students there. More would arrive later, when classes were closer to starting. However, Jessi wanted to get to class early. And her reason was simple. She wanted to spend more time with Cole. Their weekly time together was limited to the class they shared together and the extra bit of time before that class. That was why Jessi ate breakfast at a time when the dining hall mostly served the nerds who liked to get up early to start studying first thing. Or they had an exceptionally early class.

"I've got my class with Cole first. He's usually early, so we make out and pass the time in the hallway first."

It was important to note that Jessi made no mention of what class she shared with Cole. Not only had she forgotten the name of the professor, but she did not even remember what the class was for anymore. Just thinking about that class was enough to get her thinking about Cole. And Cole was a distraction that pushed out all other thoughts from her mind.

"After that," Jessi continued, "I'll just go about my day, probably trying to find a hot guy to fuck. Cole gets me so worked up. My last class before lunch is with Professor Wright. I'm not sure what he'll have for me, but I'm excited."

Candi shushed Jessi at the mention of Professor Wright. "We should probably come up with some other way to talk about him and your arrangement."

"Oh," Jessi said as she sat back, considering Candi's

words. She immediately saw Candi's point. Professor Wright was already being careful with his communications with her, using a burner phone to contact her. She needed to be equally as careful for his sake. She was happy to meet with him for sex in exchange for not having to worry about her classes or grades. However, if other students who were not as accepting found out, they could throw a wrench in the grand plan. Professor Wright could even get fired.

"I'll think of how we can talk about it while you're in class today," Candi offered.

Jessi nodded her head, thankful that she would not need to worry about that. Of course, she did not realize how she had just given up her control over the situation, instead letting Candi handle even simple details. Yes, it was easier that way, but it was the first step down a slippery slope that included a loss of control.

"Thanks for coming to breakfast with me," Jessi said when she finished her meal. "I'll see you at lunch."

"Have fun with Cole," Candi offered, taking a little longer to finish her meal than Jessi. Then again, Candi did not have the same urgency to get to class as Jessi did.

And as Jessi hurried off, Candi had to admire how far Jessi had come already. She looked completely at home wearing a cropped top and short skirt. The heels were taller than Candi had figured Jessi would choose to wear, but that definitely was not a bad thing. Jessi had definitely embraced her new role as a hot slut, but the potential for more was right there for the taking. Candi licked her lips, imagining what kind of woman Jessi would be at the end of the school year.

As for Jessi, she bit her lip as she imagined all the amazing ways Cole could make her feel good. The walk to her first class was not long, but it was long enough to give her time to think about him. This time she had not bothered with a backpack or any note taking supplies. She just had her purse. If all went well, she would not need more than that again. She was free to explore her new urges. And given the wetness between her thighs, her current urge was for sex and whatever Cole was willing to give her. She hoped it was something good.

ENJOYING LIFE

Jessi was first to the hallway outside the classroom. However, her wait was short-lived. Cole arrived after only a few minutes. And that had given Jessi time to double check her makeup and generally make sure she looked as sexy for him as possible. The moment he laid eyes on her, she knew she had chosen everything about her appearance correctly. HIs eyes traveled her body up and down, clearly enjoying what he saw.

The short skirt was a big hit, especially the way it threatened to reveal her modesty should she move too quickly or give him a twirl. Her top was as low-cut as was possible without her bra showing and it was heavily cropped, revealing her tight midriff and the belly-button piercing that was a highlight of her appearance.

"Fuck," Cole said, his voice husky. He quickly approached and ran a gentle hand down Jessi's face.

Her eyes trailed over his body, wishing she got to see him without his shirt off. That was one thing she had missed in their interactions thus far and she desperately wanted to run her hands across his bare chest. He was so strong, so handsome, so hot. Already her own arousal was taking up the bulk of her thoughts. All she could think about was him fucking her, him using her body for his pleasure. His pleasure would result in her pleasure and just being near him was enough to turn her on beyond belief.

The moment he crushed his lips against hers, Jessi let herself completely collapse into his grasp. She pressed her nubile body against his own, practically dry humping his body as he pressed her up against the wall.

"Please," Jessi managed to beg, her voice coming out in the slightest of whispers, more a moan than actual speech.

"Not yet," Cole countered, his voice hard and demanding, yet at the same time, comforting and arousing. Jessi could listen to his voice all day if she could. Whenever she was in his presence, nothing else really mattered. He was all she could think about.

One hand held Jessi's head as he positioned her to more easily kiss her. Their tongues darted in and out of each other's mouths, fully enjoying this close moment together. And from the hardness Jessi felt pressed against her, she knew Cole wanted her just as much as she wanted him. She could feel his cock pressing against her through his pants. But she still was not ready yet. He had just confirmed that. He wanted more than a slut.

Cole's other hand started to roam across her body. His fingers trailed down her arm, sending a shockwave of pleasure at his surprisingly gentle touch. He had the ability to both manhandle her and barely touch her at the same time. That alone was enough to tell Jessi that he was an accomplished lover. Once he finally did fuck her, it would be a moment she would always remember.

His hand moved from Jessi's arm to her midriff, his fingers grazing her sensitive flesh. Jessi's breath hitched in her throat as his touch, but she did not stop from kissing him. Such a thing was unthinkable, as much as she was able to think. Her whole being had been given over to the lust and arousal she felt for this nearly god-like man. That was how she viewed him, how she felt herself lucky to even just make out with him, to wait until she was ready to take the next step with him.

Cole did not care that such an open display of affection took place in public. For him, he already owned Jessi's body. She was muddy in his hands. He knew he could hit p her skirt, ditch her little thong, and fuck her right there in front of anyone who walked by. He also knew that given his position as the starting quarterback on the football team, he was not likely to see much in the way of reprimand. At most, he would probably be told not to do it again.

Not that Cole was the sort of man to flaunt such conventions. Yes, he someday wanted to fuck the little slut in his arms, but he was not about to do it in front of the student body. Although, he did hope that he would be able to make his interest in her better known soon enough. But in the meantime, he was going to enjoy himself and enjoy all the pleasure that Jessi was willing to give him.

And that included reaching up under Jessi's cropped sweater and squeezing her breasts through her bra. Even if Jessi had wanted to stop him, which she did not, she never would have dared push his hands away from her body. All it took was a kiss to drive away any sense of propriety and modesty. When it came to Cole, she was simply an object to be used. And even though every feminist bone in her body should have been screaming out against that fact, the pleasure he gave her, the way he made her feel, outweighed everything else.

Jessi lost all sense of time when she was in Cole's presence. All it took was a single hand to grace her skin, or the feeling of his lips against her, and every thought fled her mind. She simply gave herself over to the arousal and lust, letting it consume her as Cole used her body like a musical instrument, making it sing. And that was without him even going anywhere near her pussy.

And despite the long make out session in the hallway, as had become their routine, Jessi was at a loss when Cole finally removed his lips from hers and took her by the hand. He guided her into the classroom and sat her down next to him. Her eyes were glassy, unfocused. Her world had shrunk down to just Cole and herself. She neither saw nor heard the professor as he entered the classroom and started into his lecture. Nor was she aware of the other students, especially the male students who kept shooting her covert glances.

Then again, Jessi was simply lost in a different world. Cole once again placed his hand on her thigh, making the subtle statement that he was claiming her, at least while they were in the classroom together. In reality, he enjoyed hearing about her escapades around campus, sleeping with men she barely knew, if at all, sucking men's cocks. And if the rumors he had heard about her hooking up with a professor were true, all the better. All of those experiences would help shape her into the woman he knew she could become.

Jessi simply looked at Cole with a coy smile, alternating with biting her lower lips. She did not dare touch him as he paid attention elsewhere, but she only had eyes for him. And his hand on her thigh only got higher and higher as the class period wore on. As his fingers neared the junction between her legs and her thong-clad pussy, she started to squirm. Jessi could not help it. Her body was no longer completely under her own control. Cole had reached her most sensitive area and she wanted him to go further.

But Cole kept her on edge, never giving her the satisfaction or relief she so desperately craved. Not that her screaming out in orgasm would have been the proper thing to do in a classroom full of people, but Jessi was beyond such reasoning. She was horny and she needed to cum. And if Cole made her cum, all the better. It would only further cement the relationship they had forged since their opportune meeting outside the student store.

And then it was all over. Jessi found herself dazed and confused as Cole's hand slipped out from between her legs. He was packing up, leaving her.

"Fuck," Jessi moaned, her voice barely a whisper.

Jessica would have been furious to see herself this worked up over a man, to see her placed on display, to have a fellow student nearly finger her in front of a classroom full of people. But Jessi did not care about any of that. Her singular purpose was to be woman enough for Cole. He clearly liked the slutty side of her. He clearly liked seeing her dress in revealing clothing and basically throw herself at him. Then again, what man would say no to that? Still, she was determined to win his full affection.

"I'll see you later, babe," Cole said as he picked up his backpack and walked out of the room.

Jessi sat there and watched him leave, her eyes first focused on his wide and muscular shoulders. Then her eyes dropped to his ass. She had never paid attention to his ass before. Even while he was on the football field, she had not been that focused on it. But he had a nice ass, firm and muscular. How she wanted to wrap her legs around that ass as he pushed his rock-hard cock into her wet and waiting pussy. That was what she wanted. It was what she needed.

Eventually, however, Jessi managed to return enough to her senses to start toward her next class. She paused first, however, to check her hair and makeup. After what had happened with Cole, her appearance would need a little extra help. Luckily, all she really needed was a fresh coat of lipstick. Her hair and the rest of her makeup was in good enough shape to make the trek to her next class for the day.

Unfortunately, there was no soccer player for her to pull into an empty classroom to get the relief she so desperately needed. When she arrived at her next class, still late, she simply sat down in the back and stared off into space, not paying any attention to what was happening around her. She was too horny to think straight still. It was just easier to daydream about Cole and what it would take for him to finally fuck her. It was all she could think about.

Jessi's second class of the day went by in a flash. She did not even realize the class was over until her daydreams were disrupted by students collecting their notebooks and back-packs and making their way out of the door. The sounds of students preparing to leave were surprisingly distracting. Jessi found herself filing out with them, her ass swaying as she walked without even consciously thinking about it. It was a byproduct of her arousal. She placed herself even more on display.

When Jessi arrived at her third and final class of the day, she gave Professor Wright a wink as she took her seat. Now slightly more in control of herself, she selected a seat directly across from the professor, wanting to put herself on display for him. She was not going to give any hints at what they got up to outside of class, but she was going to enjoy turning him on in the classroom, making him squirm, much as Cole had made her squirm an hour earlier. The only difference was Jessi was not going to touch him, yet.

However, it did not take long before Jessi felt a buzzing in her small purse. She had not bothered to bring any school related supplies with her. She had no need for a backpack anymore. Her sole purpose of coming to class was to look pretty, flirt with Professor Wright, throw herself at Cole, and possibly collect phone numbers of other students for hookups later.

Not caring what was happening in class and certainly not listening to one of her fellow students prattle on about whatever the current class discussion revolved around, Jessi pulled out her phone to see a message from Professor Wright. He was using his burner phone in class. However, the length of the message made it clear he had written it out before class. He had only waited until now to press send.

Jessi glanced up and her eyes met Professor Wright's for just a moment, enough to know that he wanted her to read the message right there. Yes, her pulling out her phone in the middle of class and further ignoring her classmates was an insult to them, but then again, Jessi was now in a special position. Her attention or even her presence was no longer required. She was here just for the fun of it and getting messages from the professor in the middle of class was definitely fun.

She read the message, finding out all about Professor Wright's plan for her. She squeezed her legs together as she read, getting hotter at his latest designs for her. He had set up an online shopping account. His credit card was already added and he had made a wish list of items for her to purchase for herself. Jessi bit her lip as she imagined what kinds of outfits he might like to see her in. Were they just for their weekend rendezvous or did he want to see her wear them in class as well?

Jessi looked around her, figuring out if anyone was paying attention to her. The male students were, but they were sticking to covert glances that were becoming less and less covert as the class period continued. Still, no one was in position to see her phone screen.

Jessi clicked on the link, excited to see what had been chosen for her. But just as the screen loaded on her phone, a voice broke through."Jessi, can you tell us what you think of Zach's point?" It was Professor Wright. He was teasing her.

Jessi looked confused at first. Then the confusion turned to worry. How was she supposed to answer the question? Was this a test or did Professor Wright intend to draw her into the class discussions despite their deal together?

WISHLIST

Jessi looked from Professor Wright to Zach. She was only vaguely aware of who he was. Zach was not someone she would regularly associate with now. It was not that he was nerdy, which he definitely was. Jessi had no issue with nerds having once been one herself. It was that he seemed barely able to take care of himself. His pinched face was curtained by long unkempt and oily hair. She could barely see any skin on his face between his oversized and thick glasses and the scraggly beard.

However, despite Zach's appearance, the way he held the book they were discussing in his hands, as well as the amount of writing in his open notebook, told Jessi that Zach was probably a smart guy and he was probably right about whatever the class was discussing. And Jessi definitely had no clue what the discussion was about. She had not opened a book all week and she had no intention to do so anytime soon.

"I agree," Jessi finally answered. "Totally. Like, I think Zach is 100 percent right."

A few chuckles sounded through the room, telling Jessi

she might have made a mistake. Jessica would have been furious to be laughed at about such a mistake, but Jessi just brushed it off. The fact was, she did not care whether her classmates thought she was smart or dumb. She had a new calling now. And class discussions were not part of that calling. All she wanted was to be the hottest and most popular slut on campus and to finally get with Cole. Those were her two goals. Nothing else really mattered.

"Yes, well, Zach, it looks like you have at least one person in your camp," Professor Wright said, teasing his student. "But somehow I doubt that agreement will help your score with the ladies."

Zach's shoulders slumped as the professor's words sank in. He had not realized his opinion was not widely held. And the fact that Jessi had already returned to looking at her phone gave him little hope that she was actually in his corner.

Then again, Zach had no idea what was so pressing on Jessi's phone. He, like the rest of the students in the class, did not realize the special relationship Jessi had with Professor Wright or that she was looking at the wishlist he had created for her to buy clothes and other accessories from.

Jessi went back to biting her lip, her legs pressed together to keep her free hand from working its way under her short skirt, as she scrolled through the different items Professor Wright had picked out for her. The first few items were normal enough, although they definitely fit his sexy school-girl interests. They included tight and cropped blouses, little ties that were supposed to go around her neck and sit in her cleavage, as well as plenty of short tartan skirts in various color schemes.

But there were other items that fit the sexy schoolgirl theme as well. There were stockings and knee-high socks. There were also an array of shoes that fit the theme as well, all of them with high heels that never would have passed as part of a school uniform, but that was kind of the point. Every item on the list would have failed.

However, Jessi quickly began to realize that Professor Wright had spent a long time putting the wishlist together. And there was far more than just sexy schoolgirl outfits to choose from. He had a whole set of tastes that Jessi could only have imagined before. He included gags of all sorts, which were not exactly something that Jessi was familiar with. There were ball gags, ring gags, and even a gag with a fitting that was shaped like a cock so that she could suck on it while gagged.

Even with her pressing her thighs together, Jessi could feel the wetness in her panties and the cool air of the classroom cutting through the thin and now soaked material of her thong. The short skirt played a role in that. It slid up until her little wisp of underwear remained just barely out of sight. Not that anyone could see under the table where she sat, but just because people could not see did not mean there was no airflow under there. And that she could feel through her soaked panties.

As class started to wind down, Jessi had already added several items to the cart. She felt strange buying clothing and accessories with Professor Wright's money, even though he had picked out all the items and had given her instructions to do so. She still felt like she needed his approval. It was his money, after all.

Jessi was still scrolling through her phone when the students around her started to pack up and leave the classroom. Class was over. But Jessi did not move to follow. Instead, she continued to sit there, not really paying attention to the goings on around her. Her focus was on her phone as she continued to decide if there was anything else she should add to the digital shopping cart.

"Do you know what you agreed with earlier?" Professor Wright asked once the two were alone.

Jessi looked up and it took her a moment to even register that she had been asked another question. She shook her head, letting her blonde hair fall in front of her face as she did so. Jessi then used long-nailed fingers to push her hair behind her ear on both sides.

Professor Wright smirked at her response. She had no idea she had agreed with beliefs that most people on campus would decry as sexist and misogynistic. Then again, the way Jessi presented herself, it kind of made sense. However, it left the professor wondering if word of her agreeing with Zach would ultimately change her reputation. More likely, people would assume she was dumb and was not paying attention. He knew the former was not true, but she definitely had not been paying attention. And for good reason.

"Have you selected anything from that list?" he asked as he collected the books in front of him and slid them into his satchel. Unlike Jessi who no longer needed to worry about carrying books or notes around campus, it remained a necessity for him as a professor. Maybe someday he could teach without books and notes, but that would be a long time away. And he doubted that he would be able to have a relationship like the one he had formed with Jessi when he was that old.

"Do you want to see it?" Jessi asked, holding out her phone.

"Surprise me," Professor Wright answered. "But make sure you use it for our next meeting." His words were purposefully cryptic, just in case there was someone within earshot. He did not want to be overheard and then lose his job.

"Yes, Professor," Jessi agreed as she pushed the checkout button. To her delight, her school address had already been entered for her. She just had to confirm the purchase one last time.

Professor Wright watched her make the purchase and smiled. His latest plan for her was going perfectly. He was going to enjoy this new relationship with Jessi to the fullest. Sure, it would cost him money, but that was only fair. It was an entertainment expense that he was gladly willing to pay.

"Would you like to come back to my office to go over today's lesson?"

Jessi's eyes lit up with a mix of excitement and lust. "Yes, Professor. I definitely need help understanding the lesson."

The pair walked to Professor Wright's office together. Any outside observer would have no idea what the relationship between the two were. As far as anyone else could detect, they were simply a professor and student walking toward the professor's office together. Yes, Jessi was dressed like a slut. Her high heels and revealing outfit were completely unneeded for a day of class, but that was how Jessi now dressed regularly. She looked like herself.

However, as soon as they reached the professor's office, he closed the door behind them so they could have some privacy. Jessi placed her purse on a chair and turned to look at Professor Wright. Her eyes, her body language, her expression, all conveyed one question. How did he want her?

The professor circled around his desk and sat down in his chair. He let his satchel fall to the side, landing on the floor and leaning against a nearby file cabinet. He looked up at Jessi and tried to decide what was appropriate for a Monday lunchtime fling. As much as he would love to fuck Jessi's nubile body again, the risk of getting caught was too high. He would save the actual fucking for when she visited him at her house. At least that was until she had an appropriate gag to make sure screams of pleasure did not give them away.

"Get down here and suck my cock," Professor Wright

ordered as he opened his fly. By the time his cock sprung free, Jessi was already between his legs, on her knees. Her eyes were focused on the bobbing cock, her tongue darting out and licking her lips. She liked this. She liked sucking cock. It was clear as day to him. And it gave him an idea.

Jessi managed to produce a hair tie and quickly pulled her blonde hair back into a ponytail, making sure it would stay out of the way. She wanted to limit the amount of fixing her appearance she needed to do before leaving. After all, she still needed to meet her friends for lunch. A load of cum, while delicious, was not enough to sustain her, even if she wished it was.

However, Jessi needed no further prompting before she began. Without another word spoken, she wrapped her painted lips around the head of Professor Wright's cock and began to suck.

"Oh fuck, that's nice," the professor said as he leaned back and enjoyed the pleasure Jessi mouth provided him. It had only been a few days since the first time he had experienced her mouth and he had to admit, he thought she was getting better. Then again, he had no idea how short of a time she had been able to call herself a cocksucker. "Go ahead and play with yourself. I want us to cum together when it's time."

Jessi's hands immediately shot down between her legs. She pulled her short skirt up and mashed her fingers down under her thong. Jessi's eyes rolled back in her head as she looked up at Professor Wright's face. Already she could feel herself getting close to orgasm. Her arousal had come down a little since Cole had left her a lust-ridden mess, but she was still plenty horny. Then again, Jessi had found she liked being horny. She liked feeling constantly aroused. It was strangely comforting while she pushed her limits with everything else.

But as Jessi did her work with a level of expertise that belied her actual experience, Professor Wright began to imagine what it would be like if they did not need to do this behind closed doors. No, he could never allow people to find out what they were doing together, even though he was sure there had been other professors with similar relationships with students before, but there were still ways to increase the risk of exposure without making it obvious what was happening.

"I think I need a new desk," Professor Wright suddenly announced. "It needs to be something that you can fit under without being seen from anywhere but here behind the desk."

Jessi heard those words and something inside her jumped. Her blowjob was not affected by it, but Jessi had a visceral reaction to the proposal. She was smart enough to understand what the professor was proposing. He wanted to be able to have her suck him off while the door to his office was open. He wanted to be able to meet with other students and professors, at least on a drop-in basis, while she was dutifully under his desk, sucking his cock like a happy little slut.

It took a moment for all of that to sink in. And rather than be wary or even disgusted by the proposition, Jessi found herself almost purring in response. Her folds grew more slick as her body responded with another boost to her arousal. At this rate, she did not know if she would last until Professor Wright finally came. He truly had an amazing mind for their relationship and she was all for it. But there was no way she could stop herself from cumming when it came. She no longer had the ability to hold back. She was beyond the point of no return.

Luckily, Professor Wright was nearing that himself. Spending the previous class period teasing Jessi and watching her as she perused the wishlist he had made for her had turned him on more than he would have liked to admit.

Jessi hit almost all of his buttons. He knew he could never have her for himself, but the way she dressed, the way she wore her hair, the way she sucked his cock, was more than he could have imagined before she fell into his lap.

The only thing really missing in his mind was her tits. They were tiny. Not that he would ever bring up her getting a boob job. It was one thing to have her show up at his house wearing sexy schoolgirl outfits and wearing a gag with a little cock on it for her to suck on while he fucked her, it was another to permanently alter her body to his preferences. She had three, maybe four, years left at Thatcher College. Then she would either graduate or simply move on. And that was assuming she did not drop out before then. After that, she would go off into the real world as a stupid slut and he would still be teaching, hoping to spot another hot little slut he could mold to his whims like her.

"Here it comes, you slut," Professor Wright groaned as his cock surged with his seed.

The moment the sticky white cum hit the back of Jessi's throat, her fingers pushed her over the edge. She came too, her orgasmic screams muffled by the cock she continued to milk in her mouth. For Jessi, it was a level of relief that she had desperately needed. Her whole body shuddered as a cascade of orgasmic pleasure washed over her in wave after wave. And all the while, she savored the salty flavors of Professor Wright's seed as it flowed across her tongue.

When Jessi was done, she pulled back and looked up at the professor. She was waiting for something. She needed approval for what she had done, proof that she had done a good job, that she was a good cocksucker.

"Good job, Jessi," Professor Wright said. "Now get yourself cleaned up and I'll see you Wednesday in class."

As Jessi got up, released her hair from the ponytail, and applied a new coat of lipstick, the professor sat back and planned his request for a new desk. His was still in good shape, but he was sure he could find some way to "break" it.

Once done with her makeup, Jessi blew her benefactor a kiss and then shuffled out of his office. She needed to get across campus and join her friends for lunch. It had been a good start to her week so far and Jessi was certain to continue enjoying herself. But her mind was already on what she was going to do next.

INTERRUPTED PART 1

The cool air of the morning had transformed into a warm day. Fall was fast approaching so cool and eventually cold mornings were to be expected in time. But the warmer air, along with the bright sun, added to Jessi's smile as the day progressed. Even as Jessica, she had never smiled so much on a Monday afternoon, knowing the rest of the week still lay ahead with classes and the rest of college life. But now she was Jessi. Sunny and warm afternoons were for enjoying. And Jessi made sure she enjoyed everything about her day.

After filling Candi in on the sordid details of her morning, including the Professor Wish List which would help to expand her wardrobe and collection of accessories, the pair headed to the gym. Now, more than ever, it was important for Jessi to stay in good shape. She made the decision to not only be one of the popular girls on campus, but to give herself over to becoming the sexual creature she was transforming into. And that meant staying fit. It meant focusing on her body rather than her mind.

The first time the pair went to the gym dressed only in

skimpy sports bras and tiny spandex shorts, Jessi had felt uneasy. Now, less than a week later, she strode into the campus gym with a confidence she never had before. Candi filed in behind her, her body a little more impressive looking with her bigger tits, but somehow Jessi remained the center of attention. It was her confidence that did it. She knew what she wanted and she knew how to get it.

The student staff member behind the counter said nothing as they checked in, exchanging their student ID cards for towels. Jessi smirked, realizing that he had pressed his body up against the counter, likely hiding the bulge in his shorts from his hard-on. She knew she had done that and it felt good. It felt good knowing that her body was being looked at in a sexual manner.

"Thanks," she said, letting her tongue dart out and slightly lick her lips. The student worker gulped at her response to him. Candi followed with a giggle, nodding to him.

Jessi had no idea who the guy was. Despite being a sophomore, her knowledge of most of the student body was limited, although it was growing fast with the number of men she was regularly meeting. Only, when she was aroused enough, she tended to forget about asking for names. Not that Jessi cared about names. The Thatcher College campus was insular enough where she would work through the majority of worthwhile men soon enough. And hopefully by then she would be ready for Cole.

Walking deeper into the large gym area, Jessi made a note of who she saw and how busy it was. She was aware that the active sports teams were all holding practice. That meant Cole was probably out on the football field. And if he was not there, he was likely in the varsity sports gym, lifting weights or getting treatment. She knew she would not see him there.

"Let's get started with a little warm-up," Jessi said as she led Candi over to the elliptical trainers. She had a routine to follow and she knew how each step was important. Her workouts were a mix of cardio, stretching, and lifting weights, all at varying intensity levels.

The two roommates found ellipticals side-by-side and they started into their workout, chatting as they went along, their breathing starting to become more labored with the exertion. The pair talked and giggled with each other, making notes of the hot guys they saw working out as well as pointing out which guys were staring at them. Jessi enjoyed the attention they received far more than she had ever imagined she would. So much had changed for her.

Not that the pair looked so amazing by the end of their workout. The waterproof makeup they wore still looked good, but Jessi was growing tired and she had started to sweat through her clothing. She definitely needed a shower before she grabbed dinner with the girls in the dining hall.

"Hey, Jessi. Candi."

Both girls looked up to see Travis and a couple of his basketball teammates headed across the gym in their direction. They were just as sweaty, with Travis holding a basketball against his hip. He had just been playing a pickup game and had come to the gym to get a little lifting in. But the moment he caught sight of Jessi and Candi, he had to greet them.

"Hey, Travis," Jessi said with a smile. The earlier effort she had put in on the various machines was forgotten as her attention closed in on Travis.

"Hey, boys," Candi responded, equally interested in Travis' friends as she was with him.

None of them embraced. They were too sweaty for that. Although it was clear that they wanted to. Jessi had to hold herself back from pressing herself into Travis' other side, letting him wrap his arm around her shoulders and pulling her in tight. He was so much taller than her, especially when she was not wearing any heels. Her trainers made her several inches shorter than when she walked around campus normally.

"Jessi, I'm craving one of your blowjobs," Travis said, not trying to be subtle as he talked to her. Neither of them cared whether someone could overhear them. Jessica would have been scared out of her mind at his public announcement of her sexual prowess. Jessi beamed with pride instead, knowing that anyone who overheard them might seek her out for a blowjob themselves. Even if they were not her type, it was still good practice. "I'll even make sure you get a reward too."

Jessi was already game. Her answer would have been an obvious yes, but she also needed to check in with Candi. They shared a room and they needed to be aware of each other's schedules and needs. Jessi planned to invite Travis over to their dorm room, but that meant Candi needed someplace to go.

Candi, however, had already moved to greet the other two guys. They were tall like Travis, with big muscles and what she hoped were big cocks. And from the looks of things, they liked the idea of Candi spending some quality time with them. They were definitely not above sharing a hot piece of ass like Candi.

Overhearing everything that was being said, and under-standing what had not been said, Candi nodded her head toward Jessi, giving her silent approval. While Jessi was in their room treating Travis to a blowjob and getting rewarded for it, Candi would be with her two new friends, doing what-ever they most wanted to do. Candi was a three-hole slut and was up for almost anything.

"Swing by my room after dinner tonight," Jessi said, licking her lips fully, going into full seduction mode. Her whole posture changed as she moved to entice Travis, teasing him.

"You got it, babe," Travis said. "I can't wait."

Part of Jessi wanted her seduction techniques to be more immediate. She wanted Travis to drag her off into the laundry room or one of the sports team rooms so he could fuck her. But she needed to finish her workout. She needed to get herself cleaned up, refuel, and make herself ready for a fun night. Without schoolwork getting in her way anymore, she could fully enjoy her college experience and satisfy her sky-high libido.

And that libido was on full display when the two roommates returned to the dorms. They did not bother to shower at the gym, instead choosing to do so in their dorms instead. They had not brought a change of clothes with them to the gym, choosing to show up all ready to go the first time.

Candi pushed Jessi against the wall of the shower stall as she followed her roommate in, pulling the curtain behind her, giving them some privacy. Jessi opened her mouth and let Candi claim her with her lips as the hot spray poured down over them. Meeting Travis and his friends had turned them both on and there was no way they would last through dinner without going mad with lust.

"Fuck yes," Jessi moaned as her hands traversed her roommate's body, her fingers tracing Candi's curves. And what curves they were. Candi sported a fantastic hourglass shape, nothing too pronounced, but her tight waist helped to highlight the size of her tits and her wide hips. In comparison, Jessi was a stick. But that comparison did not matter, especially when Candi pushed her tongue into Jessi's waiting mouth.

"You're such a hot fucking slut," Candi countered as her hands moved across Jessi's hot skin. One hand kept her pinned to the wall while the other grazed across her belly and then down between her legs. Jessi was completely bare down there, matching Candi's own smoothness. The only hair either of them sported was on their heads. Everywhere else was smooth.

"Always." It was a commitment from Jessi. This was who she was now and this was who she was always going to be. She was a slut. There was no going back. Jessica might try and rear her nerdy head, but Jessi was in control now. Jessi was going to do what her body wanted her to do. She had started a journey at the beginning of the summer and she was going to see it through.

As Jessi held Candi close, their lips almost constantly locked together, their moans ricocheting off the tiled walls of the dorm shower room, being loud enough for anyone who walked in to hear them, but not caring at all if they were overheard, Jessi moved one of her own long-nailed hands down across Candi's torso. The destination was simple. She moved to match Candi's actions, making sure that she gave just as much as she received.

"Who's in there?" It was a familiar voice, but not one that either woman could place at the moment. Not that they cared. "Are you having sex in there? Do I need to tell the RA?"

It was one of the other girls in the section. However, as much as the young woman stood there threatening to get the two roommates in trouble for being so public with their actions, she made no move to leave and get help. Instead, she pulled out her phone and started recording. Jessi and Candi moaning was not loud, but it was definitely audible over the sound of the shower.

Jessi was lost in the sensations of her body, the pleasure flowing through her, the heat gathering on her skin and penetrating deep into her core, a combination of the hot water flowing over her body and Candi's touch against her skin, feeding the growing lust. Jessica would have been terrified at the though of getting caught having sex, even more with her roommate. But Jessi owned it. She enjoyed it. This was the new her and she was making the most of her playtime with her roommate.

"Fuck, I'm cumming," Jessi cried out as her body started to convulse with erotic ecstasy. Candi looked deep into Jessi's eyes, an energy passing between them. Before either of them realized what was happening, Candi screamed out in orgasm as well, her body leaning into Jessi all the more, their hands still working feverishly between each other's legs.

The two blondes remained there, leaning against the shower stall wall for a moment as they recovered. Both of them were still horny. One orgasm was not enough, but they both knew their evening would likely be filled with orgasms. They were in no rush to tap themselves out. This moment together in the shower was just a precursor, an act to tide themselves over until after dinner. Then the real fun could be had.

"Are you two done?" It was the same voice as before. Jessi giggled as Candi pushed herself away and the pair moved to start actually cleaning their bodies properly and not just giving into the lust they felt.

However, by the time they stepped out of the shower, their visitor was gone. They had no idea which of their fellow students had stood there and listened to them fucking each other. They had no idea it had been recorded. Not that the recording was identifying in any way. Then again, had that recording made it clear who they were and if it was spread around campus, it would have been perfect advertising for men and women, telling everyone that Jessi and Candi were hot sluts. As if they needed such advertising.

Jessi and Candi each wrapped a towel around their bodies, although they were slow to fully cover themselves, instead preferring the nudity. However, they both knew they could not return to their rooms in the buff. Their hair dripped down, darkened from the water, but still clearly blonde. Jessi spotted herself in the mirror and wondered when she would need to make a salon appointment. Going blonde required upkeep and her roots would start showing soon enough, if they had not already.

"Let's get ready for dinner, slut," Candi said with a smile.

Jessi smiled and nodded, taking her roommate's name calling as a compliment. She was a slut and she loved it. But her night had not even started yet. She still had Travis visiting and she could not wait to find out what her reward for another blowjob would be. He could definitely fuck her, but there were so many other possibilities. Jessi bounced with excitement, her arousal already growing again, ready for whatever the night brought her.

INTERRUPTED PART 2

Jessi had the hardest time figuring out what she wanted to wear for Travis that night. Part of the problem was she did not know what she was going to be asked to do with him. A blowjob was expected. She knew that. But what kind of reward did he have in mind for her? That was the question and it burned through her mind, making it hard to make decisions about what she was going to wear.

There were a few givens, of course, One, Jessi lived in crop tops now. She had no idea what she would do when the cold weather set in and she was walking to class in below freezing temperatures. Not that the walk was long. She could handle the cold for a few minutes at a time. And that was assuming she was still attending classes. For all she knew, she would spend all of her time with Cole and leave him to go to class. She could just stay back and focus on looking pretty for him.

"Focus," Jessi chastised herself as she stood in front of her wardrobe. She really wished her closet in her dorm room was bigger. It was already overflowing with clothes and she knew she had more on the way, clothes she had ordered from Professor Wright's secret wish list. Jessi had no idea what she was going to do, but there was no way she was going to stop buying new and sexy clothes to wear. She was already addicted to the feeling of adding to her collection.

Eventually Jessi decided on her outfit for the evening. It started with a pair of high-heeled sandals with straps that wound around her lower leg. The heels almost came down to a point, making balancing precarious in normal situations. However, Jessi was fast adjusting to the change in her footwear. In some ways, walking flat-footed was less comfortable than wearing heels, even impractical heels like the ones that now adorned her feet.

The itty bitty thong was just there to have some coverage to start out. Somehow Jessi had a feeling that her thong would be either pulled aside or pulled from her body before the night was through. But she was horny enough now, wet enough for almost anything, that she needed a little coverage down there when she went to dinner with Candi and the rest of the hot slut gang.

The wrap-around pleated skirt was short and definitely flirty. Jessi would not have been surprised if people knew she was wearing a pink thong by the end of dinner. Not that she cared. That was the fun part about being a hot slut. She could focus on looking sexy, but not care about the social stigmas that being a slut often caused in broader society. This was college and she was sure there were a lot of horny men who wanted to see her panties. They were young men, after all.

The top proved to be the hardest part of Jessi's outfit to figure out. She stood there for a long time in front of her wardrobe, trying to decide what to wear. She had not put on a bra yet, not knowing if she even wanted to wear a bra with this outfit. There were some areas where bras were ideal, but others where they simply did not make sense. Halter tops, tube tops, and anything that left her shoulders entirely bare required either strapless bras or simply going without.

"Here we go," Jessi exclaimed as she pulled out a cream-colored, fuzzy cardigan. She had not really considered it before, because it seemed like something that would be too warm, but Jessi reconsidered when she realized it would look great wearing it off the shoulder. And it would still leave the bulk of her midriff bare. It was perfect for the kind of look she was going for, which was sexy, but with an air of innocence too. Not that anyone who knew Jessi could call her innocent. She had already lost count with the number of men she had been with and it had only been a week.

Travis did not make his appearance until Jessi was returning from dinner. He was leaning against the wall in the hallway outside her dorm room, looking as nonchalant as possible. Jessi smiled when she saw him, having almost forgotten about the planned rendezvous. She had been having so much fun with her new friends that she completely lost track of time. Not that Candi had forgotten. She headed straight out after dinner, intent on meeting up with Travis' friends for her own fun.

"You are a vision," Travis said as he pushed himself off the wall and turned to face Jessi.

She bit her lip, enjoying the compliment. Jessica had never cared what other people thought of her. Neither did Jessi. But she certainly enjoyed compliments. She liked being told that she was pretty or that she was sexy. She liked being called a slut too, but that was a slightly different matter.

Travis stepped forward and pushed a lock of hair behind Jessi's ear. She looked up into his eyes and almost melted. Her body called out for far more of his touch. She wanted him in every imaginable way. Her mouth was already watering at the thought of getting his cock between her lips again.

Then his hand trailed down across her exposed chest, his fingers sliding gracefully across her skin. They found the top button of her cardigan and he started to pull at it, pulling the button free.

"I'm not wearing a bra," Jessi admitted, although she made no move to actually stop him. She had half a mind to just drop to her knees now and pull out his cock. Sure, she might get in trouble for blowing Travis in the middle of the hallway, but she had already been branded a slut by the campus rumor mill. There was more damage she could do to her reputation. If anything, such a blatant display might make her even more popular among the men on campus.

"Then we better get inside your room. I don't like to share like that."

The possessiveness of Travis' words only served to further stoke the fire that burned inside of her. Jessi quickly pulled open the door and dragged Travis inside by the collar of his shirt. She had to admit, he cleaned up really well from the man she had seen at the gym. Then again, she had been with him enough to already know that.

Once the door was shut, leaving the two coeds along together again, Travis took charge, opening his pants to free his big cock and then sitting down on the bed. He was already hard. He was already ready. And there was nothing stopping Jessi from fulfilling her part in their adventure together.

Jessi kneeled down in front of Travis and took his hard cock into her hands. She gripped his long and thick shaft and squeezed ever so slightly, eliciting a deep groan of pleasure that rumbled in his chest. Then she parted her lips and took him into her mouth, giving him every ounce of attention that she could manage, giving her best blowjob, hopefully ruining blowjobs for him that came from any other girl, slut or otherwise.

Jessi worked her magic, bobbing her head in his lap, looking up at him through her thick eyelashes, playing up the submissive act to the best of her ability. And then she went deep, his cock pushing into the back of her throat. She opened to him, taking his entire length into her until her nose was pressed up against his body.

"Holy fuck," Travis groaned. "You keep getting better and better. And I already thought you were the best cocksucker on campus."

Jessi smiled inwardly at the compliment. She was not sure if he was just saying that or if his cock had been sucked by the other sluts on campus regularly. Not that it mattered. She was proud of the work she had done to get better at sucking cock and even with such a strong compliment, she was not about to sit back and rest on her laurels. She was going to keep practicing, keep getting better. It was not enough to just give the best blowjobs on campus. Thatcher College was small. She had bigger aspirations, especially if she wanted to be with Cole.

Jessi took her time as she worked Travis' cock with her lips, tongue, throat and her hands when she needed to. But even he had his limits. He let out an animalistic roar as he finally came, dumping his load into Jessi's mouth, feeding her the dessert she so desperately desired. She swallowed down his spunk with gusto, making a big show of it. Travis seemed to like that too, because his cock gave a twitch in her hands, trying to come back from the orgasmic abyss. But he would have had to be superhuman to be ready to go again so soon.

"Fuck, that was nice," Travis said as he leaned back and looked up at the ceiling. He felt drained in a way that he had rarely experienced before. That was a testament to Jessi's prowess as a cocksucking slut.

But that was not enough for Jessi. She knew Travis had

something special planned for her and now she wanted it. She wanted her reward.

"What do I get now?" Jessi jumped up onto the bed, still on her knees. The excitement on her face was clear. She looked like a kid on Christmas. She could not help herself. Her whole body almost shook from it.

Travis smiled as he pushed himself back up to sitting. "Let's get you out of those clothes and then you'll get your reward."

Jessi had never stripped so fast in her life. She pulled off her cardigan top without a second thought. Her skirt came next. It was so easy to take off too. That left her there in her thong and heels. She reached down and started fiddling with one of the straps on her shoes.

"Leave those on, but ditch the thong," Travis commanded.

Jessi nearly swooned at his decisiveness. He knew what he wanted and she knew there was nothing that was going to stop him from getting it. There was nothing she could do but to just follow his directions and do as he said. She was pretty sure she was going to like it too.

She hooked her thumbs into the waistband of her thong and started to slide them down her legs. But then Travis grabbed her by the shoulders and pushed her down onto the bed. With her thumbs trapped, she was completely at his mercy. She squealed as she hit the bed, her head landing on her pillow. But she was not upset. She was still excited. This was new and fun and she was all for new sexual experiences.

Travis reached forward and grabbed Jessi's thong. He pulled it the rest of the way down her legs, pulling the flimsy bit of fabric and lace over her heels and then flung it across the room. Jessi would not be needing it again for a while. At least he had not ruined the pair. Thong replacement was becoming a thing she needed to consider.

Jessi still did not know what Travis had planned for her.

She squirmed on the bed as he positioned himself between Jessi's legs. She briefly wondered if he was ready to fuck her, but as he spread her legs and leaned it, his intentions became far more clear. He was returning the favor, using his mouth and tongue to get her off in the same way that she had gotten him off.

"Oh my fucking god," Jessi called out as her hands grabbed onto the bedding beneath her. The jolt of pleasure that shot up her spine from her pussy when Travis' tongue first made contact was enough to send her eyes rolling up into the back of her head. She had never felt anything quite like this before. It was exquisite. It was more than she had ever expected. And it was clear that Travis knew exactly what he was doing.

But then came the phone ringing. Jessi cursed as she flailed her hand around, trying to find her phone. Some-where along the line, she had set it down on her desk, beside the head of her bed. She reached out for it, intending to silence it. But then she saw the name on the caller ID. It was a call from home.

"Shit, I've got to answer this."

Jessi expected Travis to stop as she answered her phone, but he kept right on going. He might have slowed down a little, not wanting to make Jessi sound too overly sexed, but he was not going to stop unless she told him to stop.

"Hello?" Jessi said into the phone as she pressed it to her ear. She bit her lip as she tried to avoid giving any hint as to what was happening between her legs. She did not want that information to make it to the other end of the line.

"Hey, I'm good," Jessi said a moment later, her voice coming out far more breathy than she wanted, but there was no helping that with Travis' talented tongue working away. And even though she knew she could tell him to stop, she did not want to stop feeling this good, phone call or no phone call. "Yeah, school's been keeping me really busy. That's why I haven't called."

The truth was, Jessi had completely forgotten to call home as she usually did. She had been too caught up in her new life as Jessi. She had completely forgotten about trying to maintain the ties that Jessica did naturally. Jessi had no idea how everyone would react to the new her when she went home for breaks. And that was if she went home. Somehow, she had a feeling that Professor Wright might want her to stick around for the breaks. There was the week over Thanksgiving and four whole weeks in the winter. That was a lot, but she kind of liked the idea of being his plaything for a week or even longer, at least to try out that kind of life-style. Jessi was still experimenting.

Jessi let out an involuntary low moan in response to Travis' continued ministrations between her legs. It happened before she could even begin to stop it.

"What? Oh, sorry about that. I just got back to my room and sat down. I've been on my feet all day, you know." It was the best Jessi could do to cover for the fact that this phone call had just interrupted an important moment between her and Travis. She was trying to end the call as soon as possible, but it was hard to do that when her mind was so clearly divided over what she wanted. It was hard to think with the bursts of pleasure that continued to light up her body, exploding in her mind with every lick of Travis' tongue.

"Look, I've got to go," Jessi finally managed to say. "I've got a lot of work to do. And I've got a study partner here. I'll talk to you later, okay?"

Jessi hung up as soon as she could. Then she looked down at Travis' head as he continued to lick away at her pussy. She giggled, imagining Travis and her studying together. It was completely surreal and impossible to imagine, but then again, her brain was so full of endorphins and other pleasure hormones that there was no way she could even hope to do any studying. Sex was the only thing on her mind and that was how she liked it at the moment.

However, this was another reminder that Jessica was still needed. Jessi could not banish her entirely. There were certain areas of her life that she needed Jessica. Dealing with people at home topped that list. But that conversation could come another time. The phone call was over and Jessi's first man had his tongue buried in her pussy, giving her pleasure she did not know was possible. This was a good night and it was only getting better, despite the interruption.

When Jessi finally came, she ran her hand across the top of Travis' head, pulling him closer to her pussy. But he did not stop as she shook from her latest orgasm. He kept going, keeping her primed and ready. After all, she had sucked his cock more than just this once. He wanted to give her an orgasm for every one that she had given him. It was only fair. And if Jessi could not think straight by the end of the night, all the better. That was how she liked to be anyway. She liked playing the part of the brainless slut, whether she understood that yet or not.

HELPING A FRIEND

"Can I come over?"

Jessi didn't know what Elsa needed from her text, but there was no way she was going to turn down her friend. And it was not as if Jessi had anything specific going on. It was a Wednesday night and she had not lined up any action for herself. Not that her day had not left her wanting. Jessi was not ready to call herself a sex addict, but she definitely had no problem finding some when she was horny.

And horniness was something that was never far from Jessi's mind these days. She had experienced some almost mind-bending orgasms in the past week, but none of them had ever completely reset her arousal to her once normal baseline. She had developed a new normal that would take a long period of abstaining from sex for her to finally break. Only Jessi had no interest in stopping. Why turn down such pleasure? There were definite benefits to being a hot slut and Jessi was living her best slut life at the moment.

"Any time," Jessi texted back, wanting to make it clear that Elsa was always welcome. As far as she was concerned, Elsa was now a part of the group. Amy might not like a townie infiltrating their group, but Elsa was planning to enroll at Thatcher as a Jan-start, beginning school between semesters. There were not a lot of students who did that, but every year there were a few. Deferring enrollment a semester was a lot easier than deferring for a whole year, although it caused a few difficulties for the college and finding housing for everyone.

Before Elsa's text, Jessi had been sitting back on her bed, looking up at the ceiling while she mildly rubbed her clit through her panties. Her shorts were unbuttoned, giving her access. She was doing that a lot lately, rubbing her clit or pussy, often both. She had not done it while in class yet, but the increased arousal helped to take her mind off the fact she did not have much to do.

With her grades now secure, Jessi had a lot of free time on her hands. And yes, she was doing well to make the rounds with the many men on campus. But there was more to life than just non-stop sex. She had to have some downtime. But that downtime left her still horny and very bored.

There was a part of Jessi that looked over at the bookshelf suspended above her desk, wondering if it would be worth it to spend some time with her head in a book. After all, she was at Thatcher to learn and not just fuck every man on campus. And a good book could definitely give her mind something to think about.

However, there was one problem with that. Jessi did not want Jessica to return. As far as she was concerned, Jessica needed to go away permanently. If she was going to fully enjoy her life, she needed to shut the door on her past self and completely embrace being Jessi. She needed to embrace being a hot slut and not concern herself with learning or anything else that Jessica enjoyed. Therefore, the books remained on the bookshelf and Jessi instead rubbed her pussy as a distraction.

Candi was not in the room when Elsa knocked on the door. Jessi did not know where her roommate had gone off to, but she figured Candi was either getting fucked by one of Thatcher College's many studs or studying. Unlike Jessi, Candi still needed to stay on top of her schoolwork.

Jessi pushed herself up off her bed and walked over to open the door. She never bothered to button up her shorts, leaving them open, her pink thong on display. Her panties matched the cropped halter top she wore. Slight jolts of pain shot up Jessi's calves with each step. She had been wearing heels so often that standing flat-footed was becoming less comfortable. Not that Jessi planned to stop wearing her heels. She had grown to love them and they definitely helped to complete the hot slut image she had fostered since the start of the school year.

"Elsa," Jessi greeted her friend with open arms. She wrapped the more endowed Elsa into her arms and placed a kiss right on her lips, in full view of anyone who happened to be walking down the dorm hallway at that moment.

It was an open mouth kiss with lots of tongue, the sort of kiss that Jessi now regularly shared with several of her friends, as well as plenty of men. Elsa let out a low moan as Jessi's hands roamed across her body. She loved men and cock, but somehow making out with Jessi in such a public spot was almost as good as being with a man. She had not intended for the night to lead to sex with her new friend, but now that it seemed to be on the menu, Elsa was not going to turn it down.

For Jessi, her actions felt natural given her elevated state of arousal. Then again, she had just spent the better part of an hour rubbing herself without ever actually pushing herself toward orgasm. She just kept herself right on the edge, finding it to be the best way to keep lingering boredom at bay. And as for anyone seeing her kiss Elsa in the doorway,

Jessi did not care. The other girls in the dorm already knew she was a slut. If anything, knowing she now swung both ways might help turn other girls toward the hot slut life.

When all this started, Jessi had no idea that she liked women. Yes, men were her main focus, but women were fun too. There was no way Jessi could ever give up cock. She needed it in her pussy and in her mouth. She even liked getting fucked in the ass, although the timing needed to be right for that. But ever since she had been with Candi, she knew there was more to life than just sex with men. Women could be just as much fun. Besides, how could Jessi turn down a little hottie like Elsa, especially when she was already so horny?

"Fuck," Elsa said, her voice thick with arousal when Jessi finally broke the kiss.

Jessi did not say anything as she stepped back, taking Elsa by the hand and pulling her into the room. The door was pushed shut a moment later, leaving the two friends alone.

"What's up?" Jessi asked, acting as if what had just happened was entirely normal. And for Jessi, her actions had been normal. This was her new normal. She wore her sexuality openly, not letting anyone or anything get her down for not only like sex, but for liking it with a multitude of partners. Jessi was a slut through and through. And if anyone had a problem with that, Jessi simply did not care.

"Rough day at work," Elsa complained as she collapsed onto Jessi's bed.

It was only then that Jessi noticed that Elsa still wore her work uniform. That right there made her feel bad for her friend. Jessi's style had changed so much since she arrived back on campus, but she pitied Elsa for having to wear such boring clothes while at work. For a store that sold club dresses and other slut-wear, the employee uniform did nothing to help sell the clothes. If Jessi were running things, she'd hire a bunch of hot girls like Elsa and keep them wearing hot and skimpy clothes that the store sold, using them as walking models of the store products.

"What happened?" Jessi sat down next to her friend and placed a comforting hand on her shoulder. She wanted to be supportive, although she knew her options were limited.

"First the customers were yelling at me for something that wasn't my fault." There were the beginnings of tears forming in the corners of Elsa's eyes. "The computer wasn't recognizing a sale price and I had to key it in by hand."

"That's awful," Jessi sympathized. "Didn't they realize it wasn't your fault? And they got their discount anyway, right?"

"Yeah," Elsa answered with a sniffle. "It all worked out all right at first, but then my boss showed up."

Jessi already lacked respect for Elsa's boss. That went back to the first time she met Elsa, when Elsa was stuck trying to get the store ready for a grand opening while maintaining a soft opening, and doing all of that by herself. Any boss worth their salt would have been helping, since it was ultimately their butt on the line.

"She started yelling at me," Elsa continued. "First she said it was my fault the computer hadn't registered the sale price, but then she started yelling at me for giving the discount when the computer wouldn't ring it up right. Everything was suddenly my fault."

"Oh, honey," Jessi cooed as she brought Elsa in for another hug. It was the least she could do.

"I should just quit, but, like, I need the money. And it's only for a few months. I'll quit as soon as I start school in January."

"It sucks," Jessi agreed. "But work is over so let's forget about how sucky it is and do something fun."

"Yeah," Elsa said, half hearted. She remained deflated from the incident, which Jessi could not blame her.

But then Jessi had an idea. They were going to get drunk and have some fun. Maybe they could find a couple guys to fuck. And if not, they could still have fun with each other.

Jessi reached under the bed and pulled out a bottle of flavored rum. She did not know where exactly it had come from, but she had spotted it earlier in the day when she went looking for a pair of shoes that had gotten kicked deeper under the bed. It was unopened and had probably been a gift from one of the guys she had brought back to the room in the past few days. At the time, Jessi had been more interested in what the man was packing in his pants than what he was holding in his hands.

She pulled the cap off the bottle and handed it to Elsa. "You get the first drink."

Elsa took the bottle by the neck and raised it to her lips, looking forward to the chance to completely forget about her bad day and instead spend her evening with her friend. She felt much better about starting school in January knowing that she already had friends on campus. Elsa took a long pull on the bottle, making sure she would get drunk as soon as possible. That was her goal.

"Fuck," Elsa said for the second time. This time, however, it was not due to Jessi's actions but simply the lightheaded-ness that followed taking a long drink.

Jessi took the bottle back and raised it to her lips. If she was going to keep up, she needed to get started on drinking.

"Hey, we should get you out of those clothes," Jessi suddenly commented. "Because fuck that uniform. We're going to get drunk and slut you up."

"Fuck yeah," Elsa called out, probably being a little too loud for the moment, and especially the place with the thin walls of the dorm, but she did not care. "Let's do it."

Elsa took another pull on the bottle as Jessi rose to start going through her wardrobe, looking for an appropriate outfit for her friend. There was only one rule that she needed to follow. The outfit needed to be slutty. Slutty was sexy and sexy was what a hot slut needed to be, all the time.

It was not long before both girls were pushing past tipsy and into the drunk category. Elsa had removed every inch of clothing she had come into the room wearing, replacing the awful outfit with a cropped top that struggled to stretch over her tits and a skirt that was short enough that she could not sit down without making it very clear she was not wearing panties. The top was one that fit Jessi perfectly, but it was a bit tight on Elsa with her bigger bust. Not that either of them cared about that. They both thought she looked slutty and sexy.

"Oh my god, I totally forgot," Elsa suddenly gasped as she looked at her phone, checking her messages. She was not about to drunk text or dial anyone, but she could not stop herself from checking her notifications.

"What?" Jessi asked. She had changed her outfit as well. Jessi rarely went the whole day wearing a single outfit. She changed often, sometimes because her panties needed changing out, since she spent so much of her day wet with arousal, but also because she was constantly trying to be as sexy as she could be for any given moment. Classes, which she continued to attend, required certain levels of modesty. But she usually felt the need to try for something more revealing by the late afternoon or evening.

Jessi had slipped off her shorts and thong, replacing them with a tight black skirt that hugged her ass. There were cutouts along the side, making it clear she was not wearing panties. She had little doubt the skirt would be bunched up around her waist later, either because Elsa and her had found men for the evening or because they were pleasuring each other. However, she had kept the pink halter top on, since it matched the skirt nicely.

"So I've got this date Sunday night and he's got a friend," Elsa explained. "I was wondering if you want to come along for a double date."

"Ooh, I like the sound of that. What time though? I've got a standing appointment with Professor Wright for Sunday afternoons."

"Oh yeah, that's right," Elsa remembered, recalling how she had helped Jessi get ready for her afternoon with the professor after spending the night in Jessi's bed. "But no, it's late. And the friend is from out of town, so it's just for the one night, if you know what I mean."

"I'm in," Jessi agreed. "And now it's time for me to repay the favor from Sunday morning."

Jessi pushed a willing Elsa down onto the bed and flipped up her skirt. They were both going to have a lot of fun, even without men to fuck them. And maybe Candi would want to join in with her strap-on when she got back. Elsa needed a girls night and Jessi was going to make sure she got that, completely. Tonight was a night of no regrets.

44

IT FITS

Jessi was in the middle of a workout at the gym when her phone buzzed with a text message. Her phone had turned into a constant hub of notifications: messages from her slutty friends, proposed hookups with various men on campus, and an increased popularity from her social media accounts where she posted pictures of herself as she went about her day. The latter was an entirely new feeling of popularity and Jessi had never known how good it felt to take a selfie. The likes and comments only served to further embolden her slutty side.

However, this text was not from her friends or any of her male classmates. This text was from Professor Wright. And the news was good. Jessi could not keep the smile off her face as she finished her workout. Candi was huffing and puffing in comparison, but she was already getting in better shape. Jessi had few doubts they would soon be on the same level when it came to their workouts, which would take away the one advantage Jessi had.

Actually, that was not true. Jessi had other advantages, like her relationship with Professor Wright. That not only meant she could slack off in her classes, but he bought her clothes too. And those clothes had just arrived.

Jessi had chosen what to buy from his wish list. She had access to that side of things, but the emails and other forms of contact went to Professor Wright. He was the one who tracked the shipping. And it just so happened to be that her first package had arrived.

It was impossible for Jessi not to be excited. She had been thinking about the package arriving ever since she had made the purchases. She had not known how long they would take to arrive. She had not bothered to pay attention to the shipping information in the same way that she stopped paying attention to the price of the items Professor Wright had selected.

"What is it?" Candi asked, her breathing heavy and strained as she tried to keep up. She was already doing better than she had during their first workout together, but it would take weeks before she was on equal footing with her roommate.

"My first shipment from the wish list has arrived."

As much as Jessi wanted to talk about her relationship with Professor Wright, she had become aware that such conversations should not be held without considering who else was around first. In their room, with the door closed, Jessi was open about the relationship, keeping no secrets from Candi and some of her other friends. But in the middle of the fitness center, with so many people around, she did not want that relationship to become common knowledge. Both she and Professor Wright would lose if the truth were discovered.

Instead of talking about Professor Wright's list, Jessi just called it a wish list. It was easier that way and Candi knew what she meant. That way they could discuss Jessi's new life without bringing unwanted attention to themselves. Not that attention was shunned entirely. Both Jessi and Candi were dressed to show off their bodies, even if it meant breaking a few gym rules. Not that anyone complained. The other women largely ignored them and the men watched them with careful interest, not wanting to get caught staring.

"That's fun," Candi commented, approving of Jessi's situation. She was not so lucky, but there was still time for her to snag a professor of her own. If she was lucky, the professor would be tenured, so there would have been less chance of him getting fired if their relationship was discovered.

Jessi nodded in agreement. It was fun. And it was going to keep getting more fun as time went on, both because there would be future orders and because it meant that Jessi got to try everything on.

The end of the workout could not come soon enough. Jessi exercised with added vigor, wanting to get through everything so that she could swing through the student union building to get her package before returning to the dorms. It left Candi breathing even harder, but Jessi's care for her roommate was overwhelmed by her desire to open that box and try on her new purchases.

There was a part of Jessi that wanted to model everything for Professor Wright on her first time trying them on, but there was no way she could wait until Sunday to try them. Plus, she wanted to make sure everything fit her before letting him see her wear them. Anything that was ill-fitting would need to be returned, which would only delay that item being available for use during their Sunday meetings.

Jessi found herself getting wet in anticipation of visiting Professor Wright at his house again. Her first visit had been unexpected, especially the way she had played the role of cock sleeve, being little more than a receptacle where he kept his cock during part of a football game. However, Jessi still enjoyed herself. And knowing that she would be regularly dressing up for the professor made it all the more exciting.

"All done," Jessi announced before she snapped up her towel and wiped the sweat from her chest. Yes, that meant she was covering her small amount of cleavage on display, but so little of her body was covered, wearing just a sports bra and a pair of tight spandex shorts that barely covered her ass, that there was still a lot of her body on display. There always was now. That was her style. She always seemed to have more skin on display than was deemed appropriate, but that was how she preferred it now.

Despite having just finished a hard workout, Jessi and Candi still looked great. The walk to the student union building was short, since the Thatcher College campus was not that large. It only took a couple minutes to walk from one end of campus to the other. And the student union building was not that much of a deviation from their route back to the dorms.

Jessi felt the gaze of other students follow her and Candi as they walked into the large brick building. They walked past the student bookstore and Jessi thought back to the first time she met Cole. She bit her lower lip as she thought back to that moment. And back to the moments since where she had given herself fully to the man of her dreams.

There was a part of Jessi that wondered if she was doing the right thing. Yes, she was fully embracing the hot slut moniker, but there were times when her two goals seemed to be incompatible. She wanted Cole. She had no doubts about that. And she understood that she was not ready for him yet. But she did not know what being ready for him entailed. She had no idea what he wanted from her and would make her ready. She wanted and even needed his guidance.

It was not love. Jessi knew that. They were not at that point yet. But she somehow knew that she and Cole were meant for each other. They both saw it. Jessica never would have noticed, but Jessi was far more aware of social interactions and the potential for a long-term relationship with him. In the meantime, Jessi would enjoy herself, exploring her sexuality and embrace this new slutty her.

Jessi's mailbox was on the very bottom row. That fact used to annoy her, but now she enjoyed the fact she needed to bend over to check her mail, putting on a show for anyone who happened to be behind her. She had to bend her knees slightly, but otherwise she focused on pushing out her ass, bending at the hips to give people a show. There was no regular mail, but there was a package slip, promising a proper package.

"Hi, I have a package slip," Jessi said as she walked up to the counter. The student working his shift looked Jessi up and down, enjoying the sight of her body. Jessi's first thought was that the student worker was a little scrawny for her tastes, but then as she continued to think about it, she decided that still would not deter her if he made a move. At the very least she would be willing to suck him off. And if his cock was big enough, she would try to get a second round out of him.

Jessica would have been terrified to even consider such a thing, but Jessi had become such a sexual creature in the past two weeks that she did not even think such thoughts were strange. Sex felt good and she had a penchant for it. There was no doubt about that. And if she enjoyed it so much, there was little reason to stop. It was not like she was addicted, although she had no interest in stopping. Nor was it hurting her progress. With Professor Wright behind her, her class load had gotten significantly easier. Everything was working out for her.

"Here you go," the student worker said, his voice nearly cracking as he handed a large box across the counter.

Jessi was amazed at the package size, not realizing just how much she had ordered. Holding the box in her hands, she could barely see over the top. It hid her smile at what was going to come next.

"Thank you," Jessi said, her voice laced with lust and punctuated with a wink. Yes, if she came across him at a party or other spot on campus, she would definitely be willing to have some fun with him, assuming he could handle her. Some men could not handle her brazen attitudes about sex. But that was no surprise. It was not like every man on campus was a hardened sex god. Many were still virgins like she had been when she returned to campus.

"You wanted to fuck him, didn't you?" Candi asked, giggling at Jessi's naughtiness.

Jessi shrugged her shoulders, which was barely noticeable with the large box in her hands. Luckily, it was bigger than it was heavy. "If we meet again I'd give him a go."

"You're such a slut."

Jessica would have been mad at being called a slut. Jessi, however, wore the title with a sense of pride. Yes, she was a slut. She was a hot slut. She was a hot and popular slut. Sure, she had given up actually learning anything in her classes so that she could fulfill her desire to be one of the popular girls on campus, but that had been her goal. She wanted this. The deal with Professor Wright just helped and even enriched her new life.

Sadly, there were no strong and burly men to carry the box as Jessi and Candi walked back to their dorm room. Jessi knew that many of those sorts of men were either in the middle of practice for one of the many varsity sports the college sponsored and those who were not involved in sports were probably working out, getting bigger and stronger.

As much as Jessi wanted to open the box as soon as she stepped into the dorm, she knew she needed to shower. She had worked out hard and there was no way she was going to try on all those clothes while still salty and slick with sweat. That was just gross. Jessi dropped the box on her bed and then started stripping out of her workout clothes. She and Candi both headed off to the showers with only towels wrapped around their bodies. However, there was no repeat of their fun together in the shower. Jessi was far too focused on her new purchases to let herself be distracted by a little shower play.

Candi held Jessi's phone, recording a video of the unboxing. Jessi was not sure exactly what she would do with the video, but she liked the idea of recording this moment, both for her and for Professor Wright, who would surely take a keen interest in how this all played out.

"These are hot," Jessi said as she pulled out several skirts first. They were of the tartan schoolgirl variety, pleated and short. Pink was a common color, but there were some nice reds and blues mixed in as well. Jessi was already certain she would be wearing at least one of those skirts to class on Friday. She knew Cole would likely enjoy seeing her wear something like that, but she also wanted to show Professor Wright, since he clearly had a thing for the sexy schoolgirl look. Jessi did too, it turned out.

Jessi did not stop at pulling out the skirts. She kept going with the unboxing, making sure to show every item to the camera so that it was recorded. Next came several tops. They were the sort that were designed to tie off below her boobs, leaving her midriff bare. White was a common color, but there were also some pinks and blues mixed in as well, perfect for matching the various skirts.

Stockings were next to come out of the box. Jessi did not have much experience with those, but she was certainly willing to learn how to best wear them. They would add a layer of class that her slutty outfits had so far missed.

Although wearing stockings that failed to disappear beneath the hem of the skirt was pretty slutty too.

There were also shoes in the box, since Jessi would need more high heels to match the school girl look that Professor Wright favored. But the real items of note were the accessories. The ball gag especially interested Jessi. She had never done anything with a gag before. She was only vaguely aware of BDSM, but she was willing to try. She was willing to try almost anything now when it came to sex. She had very few limits.

And despite having plans to model each and every outfit for the video, Jessi did not wait before she pulled the plastic packaging from the ball gag and opened her mouth.

"It fits," Candi said as Jessi pushed the gag into her mouth. She then reached back and fastened the gag behind her head.

Jessi wanted to comment, agreeing with her roommate, but there was no way for her to speak with the gag in her mouth. She felt the saliva build up behind the gag, threatening to spill out as it found the small spaces to reach freedom. She was going to start drooling soon and the only thing she could do to stop it was remove the gag. Except, Jessi was not ready to remove the gag yet. Instead, she decided it was time to try on an outfit. Her fun for the night was only just starting.

4 5

THE FIGHT

"You fucking bitch."

Those were not the words Jessi wanted to hear, especially out of the mouth of a woman she considered to be a friend.

Jessi had been minding her own business, writing an email home so that she did not suffer another interruption like she had earlier in the week. She had learned proactive communication was better than ignoring those aspects of her responsibilities. And emails were easier to fit into her busy schedule. Not that she was as busy as she would have been without her special deal. However, maintaining her status as a hot slut required a lot of work, especially for someone who was new to the lifestyle.

Not that Jessi was willing to divulge the full truth to those people who knew her as Jessica. How could she share the fact she had worked out a deal to get good grades by fucking one of her professors? How could she tell the people who were ultimately footing the bill for her education that she had all but switched majors, studying the art of sex instead of math or science or politics or whatever she had been on the path toward studying before?

Jessica had not selected a major yet. She had several promising areas of study to choose from. She had been a talented student who could have majored in almost any area of study and thrived. But now that she was Jessi, her life was different. She was still plenty smart, but she no longer needed to strive for academic excellence. Her time could be spent doing something other than studying.

However, the words getting shouted at Jessi as she tried to focus on writing home were not the words she expected to hear from a friend. Jessi had always thought she had managed to navigate the bonds of her new friendships well enough. She was still learning, having been a natural introvert before. But that was Jessica. Jessi was no introvert. She was outgoing and always focused on being her sexy and slutty best.

Jessi shut the lid on her laptop and looked up at Amy. Her friend stood in the doorway to her dorm room, fire in her eyes. Amy was dressed as she often was, wearing a cropped tube top and a skirt. Today it happened to be a pink tube top that sat low on her tits, giving a great view of her cleavage. Her skirt was made from dark blue denim and barely covered her ass. She had topped it off with a pair of wedge-heeled trainers.

Jessi was dressed similarly, although she wore a yellow halter top that left a hands-width of skin visible between the cropped end of the top and the top of her own short skirt. Jessi had opted for a circle skirt that constantly threatened to reveal her pink thong. She had been planning to get out a vibrator once she finished her email, so the thong was not long for wearing, but she had felt more comfortable wearing it while writing home. Her shoes were a pair of high-heeled sandals with a narrow heel and lots of straps criss crossing her foot.

There was nothing to do for Jessi but to stare at her friend without any comprehension. She had no idea what she had done to draw Amy's ire. Yes, Amy had bristled when Jessi had brought Elsa into the fold, but the fact Elsa had been accepted to Thatcher College and was planning to enroll in January should have made up for it. And none of that should have left her friend in a rage.

"You know what you did," Amy called out, stamping her foot in anger. Of course, all her emphatic movement did was make her tits jiggle and threaten to pop out of her tube top. Her nipples were barely covered as it was and her movements were only making it more likely that they would become uncovered.

Normally a visit like this would have turned Jessi on. Her friend was hot and she had recently discovered how much she liked women. Men were still her favorite, but it was so much fun to play with another woman who understood the best ways to provide pleasure. It was special and after sapphic fun with both Candi and Elsa, Jessi was looking forward to bringing others in the hot slut group into the fold. But Amy was clearly in no mood for that right now.

"I really don't, Amy," Jessi countered. She stood up to meet her friend's challenge, but she did not take a step closer.

"You think you can call me by my name when you don't even use your real name with us?" Amy pressed. She held out a long nailed finger and pointed threateningly toward Jessi.

Now Jessi was seriously confused. Okay, yes, she went by Jessi now instead of her real name of Jessica, but that should have been expected. Although Jessi had never confirmed it, she assumed Candi's real name was Candi. Although she had to admit it would have been hot if her roommate had always been Candi, as if her life had always been leading to the point she would become the hot slut that she was.

"My name is Jessi. I haven't lied to you or anyone else."

"No, it's not," Amy countered. Neither of them cared that they were having this argument with the door open where everyone in the area could hear them. Then again, the walls were thin enough the neighbors would be able to hear them argue anyway. "I did a little research on you. Your real name is Jessica and you're not new to Thatcher like I thought. You were here last year."

"So what?" Jessi pressed. "What's your point? I shortened my name from Jessica to Jessi because I like it better. And yeah, I'm a sophomore and attended Thatcher last year. What's your problem with that?"

Amy's anger sputtered for a moment. It was as if she had not been expecting Jessi to admit to what Amy had been so angry about. Yes, Jessi had not gone into her past, but her new friends had not asked her about it. No one had cared who she was before she showed up on the quad on move in day, joining the other popular girls for a little afternoon sun. They had accepted her and she had found friends for the first time.

"You're spying on us," Amy practically screamed.

Jessi stood there, befuddled by Amy's conspiracy theory. It was completely crazy. Jessi was not there to spy on anyone. She was just trying to be happy. And Jessi had never been happier than when she acted like the hot slut that she had become. She loved her new life. She loved being popular. She loved dressing sexy all the time, showing off her body. She loved the way people looked at her, especially the men. But more than anything, she loved the sex. It was more and more becoming her primary motivation in everything she did.

Jessi would stand in front of her wardrobe every morning and ask herself what outfit would most easily lead to her getting fucked. Sometimes she had someone specific in mind, like trying to entice Cole, even though he remained unconquerable. No matter what she did, she was not ready for him yet. It was maddening.

Luckily, Jessi had other outlets when it came to sex. The Thatcher College campus was full of hot men with big cocks. If she really sat back and thought about it, she might wonder why that was true, but she did not really care about the answer. All she cared about was that there were a ton of hot guys with big cocks that she could suck and that could fuck her. That was what mattered.

"How am I spying on you?" Jessi finally asked. The only way she was going to get to the bottom of Amy's crazy conspiracy theory was if she asked questions and used logic to reason with her. Or at least that was Jessi's hope. If Amy was completely off her rocker and had already dived into the deep end and was beyond convincing, their friendship would be lost.

"There are certain school administrators that hate us," Amy said. She had stopped yelling, but there was still emotion in her voice. "They don't like that we aren't model students. They don't like that we party all the time. They don't like how we corrupt the men, enticing them away from their studies. And so they used you to spy on us. Super smart Jessica, a shoe-in for graduating with top honors, suddenly shows up at the start of a new year and pretends to be interested in being one of us? As if. You're just here to get dirt on us so we can get kicked out."

Jessi was still confused where this was coming from, but she was starting to understand. Amy had found out about her past. She did not know how that information had been given to her. Maybe she figured it out on her own. Maybe she saw Jessica's name printed somewhere. Maybe she even looked through the freshman look book that had pictures of all of the incoming students. This was not a secret she could hide forever. She just hoped that by the time the truth came to light, she was so far entrenched in the Jessi persona that there was no hope of Jessica ever returning. She just needed more time.

"Did it ever occur to you that I was jealous of you?" Jessi asked. It was the best place to start, because it was the truth. Why had Jessica decided to become Jessi, a popular girl? It was because she was jealous of the popular girls. Jessica had felt like a wallflower and she hated it. Thus she made the changes to her life over the summer so that when she returned to campus in the fall, she could dive right in and be this new and improved version of herself. She was Jessi now and she wanted to keep it that way.

"So that's why you're trying to get us kicked out?"

Jessi immediately scoffed at the very notion of wanting to get Amy kicked out. She did not know where that idea had come from.

"No, I was jealous so I worked hard and decided to become one of you. I wanted to join you. I wanted to be a popular girl here. And when I arrived and realized that being a popular girl meant being a hot slut, I went with it. Did you know I was still a virgin when I joined you and the others on the quad on move in day?"

Amy's jaw almost hit the floor after that confession. She never would have pegged Jessi as someone who was new to sex. Even she had seen how Jessi got around. It was no secret that the new hot slut was probably the easiest girl on campus. Amy had plenty of men in her orbit to choose from, but she was only getting fucked a couple times per week. Jessi was getting fucked a couple times per day, on average, it seemed. Those were the rumors at least.

"But if you're not spying on us, why did I just get told off by my advisor?" Amy questioned. "He's threatening to put me on academic probation if I don't do better in my classes. That's one step away from getting kicked out."

"Maybe your grades need raising?" Jessi offered. "I mean, where do you think Candi is right now? She's off studying. Although I'm pretty sure she's also fucking her study partner, but I'd be doing that too if I were in her shoes."

Amy narrowed her eyes at Jessi, finding her conspiracy theory shot to hell, but still trying to salvage some of her dignity.

"But then why did I see your name in my advisor's office?"

"Who is your advisor?" Jessi asked. The truth was, she had no idea why her name would be in a random professor's office. All students at Thatcher College were assigned advisors when they arrived on campus. Eventually the students would switch to a major advisor, but that only happened when they chose a major. Jessi had a suspicion she would be choosing Professor Wright as her major advisor. Of course, that would mean declaring his subject as her major, but as long as she could keep exchanging sex for good grades, she was not going to complain. She would major in whatever he wanted as long as she continued to get access to his cock.

"Professor Johnson," Amy answered.

Then it all dawned on Jessi. She had no idea what Amy saw, but she had Professor Johnson. It was only now that she realized that he was the professor who taught the class she had with Cole. She never paid any attention. She even forgot his name until just now. She had no idea that he was Amy's academic advisor.

"You probably saw a note referring to my special situation," Jessi shared. "You remember how I made a deal with one of my professors? Well, he is arranging it so I don't have to do anything in any of my classes. I don't know how he pulled it off, but I don't even have to go to class anymore. I still do, but I haven't taken any notes since school started."

"Oh, yeah," Amy said, the final pieces clicking into place. Her anger at her friend had waned to the point it was almost completely gone. Now Amy just felt stupid. She had assumed the worst from her friend. Jessi might have rubbed her the wrong way a few times, but she had never done anything bad. She had just shaken things up among the hot sluts. But there was no doubt that Jessi was one of them. And now that she had confronted Jessi about her concerns, albeit in a way that lacked dignity, she felt more secure in their friendship.

"Look, I'm glad you came to me," Jessi said. "I'm your friend. We should be able to talk about things. Hopefully you're willing to accept me. But you should know that even if you don't, I'm not going away. Jessi is here to stay. Jessica was boring and lonely. I don't want to go back to being an unpopular introvert. I love the attention I get now as a hot slut. I love hanging out with you and the other popular girls. And I love the sex. Holy fuck, do I love the sex."

Amy smiled. She could understand what Jessi was talking about. Even though she had been at it longer, she was not as deep into it as Jessi. But they still had a lot of common ground. And even though Amy could likely call herself the hotter of the two of them, she still found Jessi hot. The overt sexuality that Jessi exerted, the constant willingness to engage in sex, was admirable. It was something to strive for, assuming she could keep her position at Thatcher secure. But maybe Jessi could help with that too.

"Come here," Jessi said, holding her arms wide.

The pair came together in a hug. But it was more than that. Jessi planted a big kiss on Amy's lips, solidifying their friendship. They could work this out.

MAKING UP

Jessi had just expected to give Amy a basic kiss. Sure, she might add a little tongue, but it was just her being friendly. But the moment their lips came together, Jessi felt a longing she had not expected. Her baseline arousal had been steadily climbing since she returned to Thatcher College. A lot of that had to do with Candi's coaching and her time spent with Cole. Also, there was all the other sex she had. It had not yet been two weeks and she had already lost count of the number of partners she had been with.

When she returned to college for her sophomore year, Jessi had thought she was straight. She still mostly was. Jessi could not imagine herself in a romantic relationship with a woman. Not that it was easy to imagine herself in a romantic relationship with a man with how many men she regularly fucked. The closest person she could think of in that way was Cole and he had told her she was not ready yet.

Given what Jessi had already done with Candi and Elsa, she now knew she was bisexual. As great as it was to get a cock in her, either to suck or fuck, Jessi saw the wisdom in sex with women. Women already knew how to best pleasure

themselves and therefore they could make great sexual partners. Men had a steeper learning curve. Women already
knew the best ways to turn each other on and to make each
other orgasm. It was wonderful.

With Amy though, Jessi felt more than just a desire as
their lips met and their bodies pressed together in a hug. She
felt something new rise within her. It was an urge to be in
charge. It was an urge to take the lead. It was an urge to
dominate.

As Amy melted into the kiss, signaling her desire for
more. And Jessi was ready to take advantage. She spun Amy
around and then pushed her down onto the bed. Amy
gasped, not in pain, but in arousal, not knowing that Jessi
could play so rough with her.

When Amy entered Jessi's room, she did so in a rage,
believing that her new friend was trying to undermine her,
to destroy her, probably out of jealousy and hatred for
popular and slutty girls. But now she saw Jessi as something
else entirely. She saw her as a beacon of sexuality. Amy had
always been popular and a hot slut. From the moment she
stepped onto the Thatcher College campus, she had been the
envy of other girls and looked upon with lust by her male
classmates. And it had all come naturally to her after a lifetime of training.

Jessi, on the other hand, was new to the hot slut life.
However, she had taken it to such an extreme that Amy knew
Jessi would soon supplant her as the hottest and sluttiest girl
on campus. It was inevitable. It might take weeks or even
months, but Amy's time at the top would eventually come to
an end. She knew it, but at the moment, she struggled to
care. Jessi's sexual nature left the hot slut enraptured. She
had been with women before, but somehow she knew this
was about to be a very different experience to what she was
used to.

Jessi went to the door and made sure it was securely closed, along with leaving a hair tie on the handle to clue Candi in to what was happening inside. The hair tie was an easy solution. Both Jessi and Candi almost always kept one on their wrists, just in case of emergencies. And slipping it onto the door handle was an easy action that could prevent an unwanted interruption later. And even though the sex might include rather loud moans and even screams, the signal itself, between roommates, was otherwise ease to miss.

When Jessi turned back to look at Amy, she saw her friend laying back on the bed, her eyes hooded in lust. It was an enticing sight, making Jessi realize that she was going to need to order a strap-on of her own, because she could not imagine a better way of dominating her friend than by fucking her with a fake cock strapped to her hips. Amy would love it and Jessi knew she would too.

"I think it's time we get to know each other better," Jessi said as she stalked toward her friend, swinging her hips and generally acting the role of seductress. It felt good. It felt right. Jessi knew she was a natural submissive, at least with men. But with other women, Jessi had started to discover that she had a dominant streak in her.

Amy did not say anything, but she nodded her head, accepting what was about to happen. This was definitely a turn of events for the woman who was generally considered the leader of the hot sluts. Amy was known across campus by almost every single person. Jessi had even known who Amy was, even if only in a general sense, back when she was still Jessica. She had seen Amy and recognized her as a popular girl, as the popular girl.

Jessi climbed up onto the bed and straddled Amy's body. She felt Amy tremble with anticipation beneath her, the slut's body almost shaking with anticipation. Jessi lowered her face, going in for another kiss.

The first kiss between Jessi and Amy had been open mouthed, but nothing extreme. This was different. Their tongues intertwined, dancings as they made out. Amy let out a delicious little moan of pleasure, the first true acceptance of the pleasure she could experience in submission to another woman. Jessi had felt that same pleasure with Candi, but the relationship between the two roommates was already starting to shift.

Jessi broke the kiss, leaving Amy panting in need. Her whole body was hot, her skin more sensitive than she could ever remember. Jessi started laying hot kisses against Amy's chin. Then she moved down Amy's jaw, toward her neck, leaving Amy to squirm beneath her. It was already too much for the more experienced slut. Her hands tried to reach her most intimate area, to touch her clit and her pussy, but Jessi's legs were in the way. They blocked Amy's access to herself, which both made Amy's need greater, but also gave the new slut even more power over the woman beneath her.

Those hot kisses continued down Amy's neck and then across her collarbone. Jessi coupled the kisses with reaching her hand down between Amy's legs. The denim skirt she wore was no barrier, lifting easily away. Jessi's fingers found a sopping wet thong, full of Amy's juices. Her friend was more than a little turned on. She was absolutely stewing in arousal, her whole body humming with need and begging for release.

"You're so wet for me," Jessi cooed in Amy's ear.

Amy let out a long moan as she arched her back beneath her friend. Her whole body felt as if it was on fire, but the pleasure was beyond what Amy had ever imagined such a recent convert to the hot slut lifestyle could provide her. She had not even imagined another woman could make her feel this way before. She was already starting to question her previously believed upon sexuality.

"But you want more, don't you?" Jessi continued. "You're just a naughty little slut who needs to cum. Tell me what you are."

"I'm a naughty little slut," Amy moaned. "I need to cum. Please make me cum."

Jessi let out a little giggle as she realized the power she now held over her friend. They had been on opposite sides of an argument just a few minutes before and now they were in the throes of a sexual moment that would redefine their friendship and their lives.

"All in good time," Jessi whispered, her wet lips grazing Amy's ear. She followed that by blowing gently on Amy's wet skin, making the slut squirm even more.

However, Jessi was nowhere near giving Amy the release and relief she sought. Bringing her hand back up from the junction between Amy's legs, Jessi pulled gently on Amy's tube top, freeing her tits. They were bigger than Jessi's small breasts. Jessi could not even call her breasts tits. They were too small for that. But Amy had a nice pair of tits, natural and big, without being too big.

Jessi renewed her kissing, working back down Amy's neck, across her collarbone, and then down her chest until her lips wrapped around a nipple. She kissed and sucked gently before blowing on the nipple. It hardened under her ministrations, Amy's sensitive flesh betraying what little control she had left.

Then Jessi started all over again, working from Amy's lips, down across her jaw, down her neck, across her collarbone and then finally to the ripe strawberry that was Amy's other nipple. It had already hardened in response, but the moment Jessi blew on the wet nipple, Amy let out a scream of pleasure that filled the room and made it clear exactly what was going on inside to all those within 30 feet, the walls doing little to dampen the sound.

Amy wiggled beneath Jessi, squirming both away from and toward the onslaught of pleasure. And as far as Jessi was concerned, she was still only getting started with her friend.

Jessi continued these ministrations, continuing to push Amy to new heights of pleasure. But she interspersed those moments of extreme pleasure for Amy with the slow disrobing of each other. Amy was lost to the pleasure and was of little help, but Jessi managed to strip her friend of all of her clothes, except her heels, as Jessi did the same to herself. It took time, removing those little scraps of clothing, but it was not long before they were both naked, their bodies glistening as nothing prevented the most intimate of touches.

Reaching down again, there was nothing to prevent Jessi's fingers from finding Amy's clit. Her hard nubbin was already engorged and primed for more. Amy let out a long moan as Jessi pushed her to new heights. And then when Jessi pushed a finger inside of her friend, all hell broke loose. Jessi knew exactly where to place her fingers, stimulating Amy's G-spot to maximum effect.

Amy bucked beneath Jessi, her mind all but shutdown under the overwhelming pleasure. "I'm coming," she moaned, her voice barely recognizable. Amy could not remember ever cumming harder, her orgasm setting off a massive cascade of erotic energy flowing through her.

Jessi urged her friend on. "Do it. Cum for me, you naughty slut. Who cares about school or grades when you can be such a hot little fuckslut?"

Amy did not answer. It was impossible for her to form any more words. She was just a vessel of pleasure, her body pushing out the ability to think. It was all only temporary, but Amy already knew, deep down, that she would be back for more. This single moment, with Jessi guiding her, had opened up a whole new world for Amy. Jessi had rocked her world and shown her new meanings for the words submission and pleasure. Amy had just relinquished her throne as the hottest slut on campus. Jessi was the new leader, even if only in name.

It took time for Amy to recover after her mind-altering orgasm. She continued to lay on the bed, breathing heavily, her chest rising and falling, her body splayed out, looking good enough to eat. Jessi rolled off her friend, but remained beside her, pushing her naked body up against her. She gently stroked Amy's hair, providing a loving moment of aftercare, cuddling up and letting Amy slowly return to full alertness.

And once Amy finally had recovered, once she was at least mostly capable of rational thought, once she could count without using her fingers, Jessi pulled away, rolling onto her back and spreading her legs.

"It's time to return the favor."

Amy liked her lips, not bothering to say anything. She had just been given the best orgasm of her lifetime and now it was time to repay her benefactor. Amy could not hope to be as good as Jessi had been, but she could try. And she was going to try her hardest to make it a pleasurable experience for the now de facto leader of the hot sluts. The other girls might not understand it yet, but Jessi had just cemented herself as the future queen. In time, all would recognize her power.

DO'S AND DON'TS

Jessi was being her sexy hot slut self once the weekend started. Much like her previous weekend, she had sucked and fucked random men at the Saturday football game. And that was in addition to her wild night of partying Friday night.

The whole night had turned into a blur as she found her way to a house party and danced the night away, only taking breaks to drink beer and either fuck or suck one of the many men at the party. It was the kind of night that Jessi now lived for, one where she came multiple times and generally had the time of her life.

It had all been so easy. Jessi had simply turned off her mind and let her body take charge. And it turned out that her body knew exactly what it wanted. The arousal she felt, the way her body had been primed for sex, was quickly becoming a new normal. And adding in the effects from the alcohol and there was nothing Jessi could do to stop herself from giving into her newfound sexual instincts.

All it took was a hot guy pressing his body against hers on the dance floor and she would happily wrap her arms around his neck or grind back against him. And she was then almost certain to drag him off the dance floor for some extracurricular fun. She sucked men off in the bathroom and found an unused bedroom to get railed hard from behind. It had been a good thing she had not worn panties to the party, because she surely would have lost them at some point during the night. Besides, panties would have ruined the lines of her dress.

But that night of debauchery was behind Jessi. She was on the precipice of a whole new night of fun. After spending her Saturday continuing to be confused by the rules of American college football, Jessi had instead focused on cheering and looking as hot as possible. She even made it on the Jumbotron at least once as she screamed and danced to whatever music was playing at the time. It was a fun afternoon, despite not understanding the game she was watching.

At least Jessi could recognize Cole out on the field. She was getting better at recognizing the players. It helped that they all had their names on the backs of their uniforms, but she was able to spot Cole even without his name being visible. And it was clear to her and everyone else in the stadium that Cole was the best player on the field. He simply dominated out there and led Thatcher College to a second win of the season.

But now that the game was over, the real partying could begin. Jessi got dolled up in a slutty little dress that barely covered her small boobs or her butt. It was pink, with large cutouts to show even more skin, including her pierced belly-button. That was one of Jessi's favorite features. She did not have the tits that her fellow hot sluts had. But she did have a tight and toned midriff with a piercing that she loved to show off.

And that was really what Jessi was all about now. She loved showing off. She loved people looking at her for her body. She loved exuding pure sexiness and hotness. Best of all, Jessi was confident that by continuing to wear revealing clothing, she would be able to keep Jessica far away. That was what she wanted. Jessica was filled with so much worry and nervousness that she could never let loose and have fun. Jessi was all about having fun. It was what she lived for.

Not that anyone but a handful of people knew there had ever been a Jessica. Jessi had done such a good job of changing her life that almost no one considered that Jessi was Jessica. Sure, Amy knew the truth, but Amy was no longer a problem for Jessi. They had made up and now it was all about charging forward into the future. And it was a future that included a lot of sex.

Jessi had barely spent more than a minute at her first party of the night when her first suitor of the night approached. She was tipsy, but still fully capable of making decisions for herself. And there was no doubt that the man was hot. One look at his strong jaw told her that this was a man she would enjoy spending time with. And the football jacket he wore told her he was on the Thatcher College team. Jessi definitely had a preferred type, and playing sports certainly fell into representing her kind of man.

"Fuck, babe, you're hot," the man said. He was confident enough in himself to not even try a real pickup line. He simply called it as he saw it and there was no doubt that Jessi was hot. While the other hot sluts might have had more attractive bodies, there was something different about Jessi. She wore her sexuality out in the open, making it clear what her intentions were. There was no doubt that she was a slut. It was practically printed on her forehead.

"You're pretty hot yourself," Jessi said, stepping forward and running her hands up the man's strong chest and across his shoulders. "I'm Jessi. What's your name?"

The way Jessi pressed herself against her latest soon to be

conquest made it perfectly clear what she had in mind with him. And the way he ran his hands over her back and down her sides was more than enough reciprocation to make his intentions clear as well.

"Ferris," the man answered.

Music played and the two found themselves swaying to the beat, not really dancing, but still moving to the music.

"You're on the football team?" Jessi asked. She had to imagine that only a football player would wear such a jacket, but it was possible he had gotten it some other way. Maybe his friend was on the team and he was borrowing it.

"That's right," Ferris answered with a proud smile. "And we won today so why don't you and I find someplace quiet so you can give me a proper reward."

It had been phrased like a question, but Jessi knew it was not a real question. It was a suggestion. And Jessi was all for it. She wanted the same thing Ferris did. It was even better that Ferris had helped Cole win the football game. Jessi might not care about the game itself, but she cared about her school and wanted to see her team win. Ferris was a part of that.

Without even waiting for the song to finish, Jessi grabbed Ferris by the hand and pulled him away. She stopped off in the kitchen where she grabbed a bottle from the counter. She did not even bother taking a look at what it was. All she knew was it was alcohol and she fully intended to keep her sexy drunken fun going for as long as possible.

As they climbed the stairs, Jessi took a swig from the bottle. She immediately noted that it was whiskey. Definitely not her favorite alcohol to drink, but it did the trick. The buzz behind her eyes grew a little stronger as she passed the bottle to Ferris, allowing him to partake.

It did not take long to find an empty room with a bed. Jessi pulled Ferris inside and shut the door. The music and general din from the party downstairs could still be heard, but at a significantly reduced volume. Jessi could actually hear herself think, not that there were many thoughts running through her head beyond the simple desire to get a cock inside of her. She was horny and wanted to fuck.

"Do you want to take it slow or fast?" Jessi asked seductively as she walked toward the bed, swaying her ass to maximum effect. She was quickly learning the art of seduction, although she still found that pure sluttiness got her what she needed. Still, it was fun to play temptress and actually seduce a man. Then again, considering the way Ferris had approached her made it clear what his intentions were. There was no need to actually seduce him.

"Fast," Ferris said. "We'll save slow for later tonight. I have a feeling that you and I are going to get to know each other really well."

Jessi giggled at the thought. She had figured Ferris would be her first of several men tonight, but if he wanted her all to himself for an evening, who was she to complain? It was rare for Jessi to have those kinds of nights, where she got to experience the same man over and over again. The last time she remembered doing that was with Christof. That had been seriously fun, although he was not enough to draw her away from the slut lifestyle that she had adopted. One cock was not enough, unless it was Cole's cock. She figured she could settle down to just one man if it meant getting regularly fucked by the man of her dreams.

Jessi climbed up onto the bed and pulled her dress up over her ass, revealing her butt and pussy to her man of the night.

Ferris took her forwardness as a clear signal of what she wanted from him. He knocked back another slug of whiskey and then pulled out his cock, leaving his pants around his knees. He could finish removing them later. For now, he wanted to sample Jessi's pussy and he could not stand to wait long enough to undress. Besides, it was not like Jessi had disrobed either. She had simply moved her clothing out of the way so that she could get a cock inside of her all the sooner.

The moment Ferris' cock entered her, Jessi screamed out as an orgasm almost took her right there. She managed to hold back, but the pleasure was already strong enough to push her over the edge. It had only been a few hours since she had last cum, but it felt like it had been days or even weeks. Jessi's body clock was off, but she did not even care about that. She just cared that there was a cock inside of her, fucking her like the slut she was.

It did not take long before Ferris had found his rhythm, pumping in and out of Jessi's pussy, each thrust making her moan in pleasure. Ferris was not the biggest man she had been with, but he knew how to use his cock. Somehow he pushed all of her buttons, giving as much pleasure as he received. And Ferris received plenty of pleasure as he fucked Jessi from behind. He had never felt such a perfect pussy in his years as a virile man.

"Ferris, what the fuck do you think you're doing?"

Jessi knew that voice right away. She had masturbated while thinking of the man the voice belonged to. She had watched the voice's owner rule the football field. It was that man she wanted more than any other. Ferris was a nobody compared to the owner of the voice that made her insides melt. Then again, no one could hold a candle to Cole.

Jessi felt Ferris go soft inside of her. She turned and looked over her shoulder to find Cole standing in the doorway, his arms around the shoulders of two girls. It seemed like he was about to hold a little victory celebration of his own. But Jessi did not understand what Cole's objection was.

He knew she was fucking around. It was a part of her preparations for when she was finally ready for him.

"I'm sorry, Cole," Ferris said, his voice lacking any hint of his previous confidence. He pulled out of Jessi's pussy and started to pull up his pants. "I didn't realize—"

"Get the fuck out of here, man," Cole shouted, interrupting. He was angry, but Jessi did not understand. It did not help that she was still horny and now no longer had a cock inside of her. She wanted that cock so she could finally cum.

Ferris bolted through the door, past Cole and his two girls for the evening, his pants still unfastened. He had to hold them up to keep them from falling back down around his knees.

"What the hell?" Jessi cried as she sat up. "I was almost ready to cum. Unless you're here to finally fuck me, you can just go fuck off."

Cole's expressions softened now that Ferris was gone. "I didn't want to interrupt, but I saw you drag Ferris upstairs as soon as I arrived. He's off limits. Or, to put it more plainly, you're off limits to him."

Jessi was pissed. She had been so close. She had held back so that she did not cum right away, wanting to enjoy the moment. But now she was sitting on the bed, her dress still hiked up over her hips, horny as all hell, and without a cock to fuck her. And it was not like Cole owned her. Yes, she desperately wanted to get together with him. She wanted to be his girlfriend, but she would have happily accepted being a one-night stand, just to sample his sexual prowess. But that did not mean he could dictate who she fucked.

"Bullshit. Why can't Ferris fuck me?"

Cole stood there for a moment, considering how he wanted to answer. "I want you sleeping around before I make my move, but there are a handful of people you shouldn't fuck. Ferris is one of those people."

"What makes him one of those people?" Jessi pressed. Her hands gripped her thighs, trying not to think about her arousal.

"He's the backup quarterback. Fucking Ferris is like trying to replace me."

"Oh." That was all Jessi could say to that. She did not really understand, but she could accept that. Ferris was Cole's backup. She could see how fucking him was a problem. "You're sure you don't want me tonight?" Jessi turned hopeful with her last question. She could dream. "I'd be totally down for a foursome. Three chicks and a man sounds really hot."

Cole just shook his head. Jessi really did not understand. What else did she need to do to get ready for him? She needed to ask him, but this did not seem like the right time. Not that their hours spent together during the school week were particularly productive in that manner either. The moment that Cole touched her or kissed her, all thoughts fled from her mind. She spent that time together in blissful happiness, letting herself become Cole's plaything.

"Go back downstairs and pick up another guy," Cole finally suggested. "Anyone but Ferris. That's basically the rule for you until I deem you ready."

"Fine," Jessi said as she climbed off the bed and tugged her dress back down so that it covered her ass and pussy. She stomped past Cole, leaving him to his fun with the two sluts he had procured for the night. From the looks of them, they were not even students at Thatcher College. But that did not bother Jessi. As far as she was concerned, Cole could fuck any women he wanted. She would always be there for him when he finally determined she was ready for him. It was just a matter of time.

4 8

THE FASHION SHOW

Jessi was still seething a little Sunday from the encounter with Cole at the party. The way she saw it, until Cole was willing to get his cock out for her, she could fuck anyone she chose. Not that Jessi had gone through with fucking Ferris. Instead, she went back down tot he party and picked up another guy, because there was no way she was leaving the party without fucking someone.

Sex that night had been different from what she was used to. Jessi's anger at Cole bled into her encounter with her next conquest. She did not even remember his name. The best way Jessi could describe it was hate fucking. She let her anger take hold and she fucked the guy hard, egging him on until he was slapping her ass and being extra rough with her. And that only made it all hotter, at least in that moment.

Looking back on last night's debauchery, the sex had not been as good as Jessi had hoped. But she also realized her displeasure about Cole's ruling colored her memories of the night. It was a night that Jessi was happy to put behind her.

Luckily, Jessi had something else to focus on. She had her meeting with Professor Wright to look forward to. She spent her morning packing up her new purchases into a bag she could carry to his house. Jessi chose one of the outfits she had ordered, a pink tartan skirt that barely covered the curve of her ass and easily revealed her lack of panties if she bent over or turned suddenly.

The white blouse was so thin her nipples could be seen through the material. It was not something she would wear to class or really anywhere else. And even as she made her way to Professor Wright's house, she wore a long coat that both concealed her top and her short skirt.

What was not concealed, however, was her shoes or stockings. The stockings were similar to the material of her blouse, thin, but with a seam up the back that Jessi worked hard to get straight. The shoes were tall, pink, platform Mary Janes. Every step came with a clip-clop sound as she walked off campus to meet with her professor.

This time there was no hesitation when Jessi reached Professor Wright's house. She walked right up to the front door and rang the bell. She was a few minutes early, not wanting to face another spanking for her tardiness. Thankfully the spanking she got in last night's hate fuck had not left any bruises on her ass. However, she was certain that another spanking certainly would. Jessi wanted to be able to sit in class tomorrow.

"Welcome," Professor Wright said with greedy eyes. Even though most of Jessi's outfit was hidden beneath her coat, he still looked her up and down, enjoying seeing her blonde hair in pigtails and the white stockings on her legs. "Please, come in. I can't wait to get started. You have no idea how much I've been looking forward to this afternoon."

"Me too, professor," Jessi said as she stepped through the doorway. Once the door closed behind her, she reached up and pulled down the zipper of her coat, revealing the outfit she wore beneath it. It had been too early to actually wear the coat, too warm out, but she had managed to make do on her walk.

"Fuck," Professor Wright said the moment he saw Jessi's nipples through her blouse. His voice was low and husky, a clear indication of just how turned on he was. Then again, all Jessi had to do was look down to see his cock tenting his pants.

"I'm wearing the clothes you selected for me," Jessi said as she set the bag down on a bench by the front door and then shrugged off the coat. Professor Wright took the coat from her and Jessi then proceeded to give a twirl so that he could see her in all her slutty schoolgirl glory. By the time she turned back to face him, it was no secret that she wore no panties. She was completely bare down below, her pussy wet and ready for whatever the professor had in mind for her today.

"It's been hard to make do with just your after class blowjobs," he admitted. "You are such a hot slut that I always want more. And seeing the way you dress in my class, watching you eye the other students, posing your hot little body for them and me, not paying attention to anything going on in class as you proposition your next fuck or browse the online shopping site I set up for you, all I want to do is fuck you and make you scream out in pleasure."

Jessi bit her lip, enjoying the compliments he gave her. Normally such words would have meant nothing to her. They would have made Jessica furious at a woman being so sex-obsessed. She would have hated it even more seeing that it was her acting that way. But Jessi took them as a compliment. She enjoyed hearing how sexy she was, how disconnected from the academic realities she was. It made her wet being viewed in such a sexual manner, knowing her body and actions were making Professor Wright hard, making him want to fuck her.

"You know, I won't be able to scream if you use the gag," Jessi finally replied. She was still unsure if she wanted to actually use the gag, but she was definitely willing to try it if Professor Wright demanded it of her. However, she hoped that by making it clear that the gag would effectively silence her during sex, he would not be able to make her scream in pleasure as he so desired.

Her professor looked at her for a moment, trying to decide what he wanted to do. He had not expected her to challenge him like that, but he had to admit that she was right. But then there was the simple fact that they had all afternoon to play.

"I think there will be opportunities for both. What do you say to that?"

A giggle bubbled up before Jessi could answer. She had been giggling more and more lately. Men seemed to like that response from her. And given her new proclivities, pleasing men had become one of her chief activities. But it was not so much the pleasing that interested her as what happened after she pleased them. That was where the real fun was, because that was where she got fucked or she got to give a blowjob.

Jessi had obviously started with blowjobs in her introduction to sex. It was something that gave her no direct pleasure, at least in the way that a cock in her pussy could give her, but she still enjoyed it. There was something special about controlling a man's pleasure, making him feel good in such a submissive act. But that act came with power. A man's cock was a delicate instrument and the mouth could provide both pleasure and great pain. The fact she chose to provide that pleasure made Jessi feel more powerful. Plus, she liked the taste of cock and cum. That fact alone was enough to keep her lips parted.

"I'll do whatever you want me to do," Jessi answered. She held her hands behind her back, thrusting out her meager breasts. She was more and more wishing she was bigger, but that was not something she could worry about now. It was out of her control. It was not like Jessi could just magically make her breasts bigger and the cost of surgery was far too much to consider. She did not have access to thousands of dollars to spend on getting a boob job.

"Did you bring the other outfits?" Professor Wright asked.

Jessi nodded her head, glancing down at the bag she had brought with her. "I brought everything that has arrived so far."

"I think a fashion show is in order."

Professor Wright led Jessi to the living room where he sat down as instructed her on what he expected of her. Jessi smiled at getting to show off. That was probably her second favorite part of being a hot slut. She loved the sex, first and foremost, but she had grown to love showing off, dressing in skimpy outfits and getting men, and a few women, to ogle her. More than once she had masturbated to the thought of wearing a particularly sexy outfit around campus and the reactions she would get from students and staff.

Even the disparaging looks she got from some of the women, women who were like she used to be, turned her on. If they would listen, she would explain to them how much happier she now was. Worrying about classes and grades was awful. It was much easier and so much more fun to instead, be a hot slut, to focus on looking sexy and having as much sex as possible.

Jessi spent two hours giving Professor Wright a private fashion show. It was broken up with a lengthy blowjob in the middle, the professor no longer able to hold himself back and Jessi more than happy to suck his cock. She was already wet as could be, turned on far more than usual, and her mouth had started to water the moment Professor Wright pulled out his cock and started to stroke it as he watched her.

Thankfully, Professor Wright was fully capable of using his cock several times in a day, because once the fashion show ended, he instructed Jessi to climb up into his lap and ride him. Jessi moaned as his cock entered her, her arms wrapped around his neck. He kissed her as she started to bounce and grind on him, her legs straddling him as she fucked him.

And those moans quickly transitioned into scream of pleasure as she rode his cock hard, her body moving to a beat only she could hear, her body aflame with passion and sexual need.

"Oh fuck," she called out. "I love your cock. It feels so good inside of me. Make me cum. Make me cum so hard."

And that was exactly what happened. Jessi came hard as Professor Wright flooded her pussy with his cum. The pair came together, the professor letting out a low groan of pleasure while Jessi screamed out as her orgasm raced through her, all of that pent up sexual energy getting released in a single moment, like a dam bursting. Jessi's eyes rolled up into the back of her head as she came, her vision turning white.

When Jessi started to recover from her orgasmic high, she realized she was still on her professor's lap, his softening cock still inside of her. That was not exactly a bad thing. His presence inside of her still felt good. She let herself rest against his chest, enjoying a moment of closeness that was rare in her usual sexual trysts.

"You are the best fuck I've ever had," Professor Wright said. "Now how about you suck my cock for a bit, getting me hard again, before we have another go. And this next time I want to fuck you with that gag in your mouth. You're going to look so hot like that, drooling and unable to speak."

Jessi dutifully climbed off of the professor and then kneeled at his feet. He left his cock out, giving her access with her mouth. She knew to take it slow. His cock would still be sensitive after cumming. But she was happy to do it. And the fact she got to taste herself on his cock did not faze her in the slightest. It only added to the taste, to the fun.

Professor Wright turned on the television as Jessi worked between his legs. He largely ignored her, although he did glance down at her occasionally, always to find her eyes looking up at him, adding to her submissive act with an appearance that definitely aided him in getting hard again.

And once Professor Wright managed to recover, he ordered Jessi to the bedroom. He had her strip off the flimsy bits of clothing she still wore and then he placed the gag in her mouth, tightening it behind her head. Her voice was cut off, but he gave her a signal she could use if she needed to stop, tapping out of the next bit of fun.

Jessi was positioned on the bed, on her hands and knees, her ass facing the professor. He stripped off his own clothes and came up behind his student, his cock hard and already glistening with more pre-cum. He was ready and so was Jessi. Her slit sparkled in the light, her wetness evident for anyone to see. She wanted this just as much as the professor did. And as she looked back over her shoulder, she could not prevent a line of drool from escaping her mouth, dripping down her chin, making her look even sexier in her professor's eyes.

The gag did not stop Jessi from moaning as Professor Wright entered her. His cock felt oh so familiar, but the gag made it all the hotter to her. And by the time the professor started fucking her in earnest, Jessi was already cumming, her body convulsing as another wave of pleasure flowed through her like a cascading wave. But the professor did not stop to let her ride out her orgasm alone. He kept going, pushing Jessi's arousal to remain unnaturally high.

Jessi had barely recovered from the last orgasm when Professor Wright finally came. His cock surged inside of her as another load of hot white cum filled her pussy, setting off her third orgasm of her visit.

This time, Jessi's arms gave out beneath her, leaving her to face plant into the pillow in front of her, her drool getting all over the pillowcase. But Jessi was unable to care about that. She could only feel the pleasure racing through her body, flowing out from her pussy in waves, filling every inch of her. And all she could do was moan. Jessi was in heaven.

It was a happy ending to her visit. Professor Wright checked on her, making sure that she was okay. Jessi was not in the mood to say much. Once her voice had been taken from her, she kind of found that she liked it that way. It forced her to put even more effort into looking seductive and sexy, using the movements of her body to take the load.

However, Jessi's day was not yet done. Even after parting ways with the professor, she still had a full card, with a double date alongside Elsa. Jessi had no idea what her evening would contain, but she was certain that there would be more fucking. There was no way she could stop at just the three orgasms from a cock. All Jessi could hope for was that her man of the night was handsome, hung, and willing to give her what she needed.

DOUBLE DATE

Jessi was buzzing with anticipation. She had no idea what to expect from her double date with Elsa. This other man was a mystery to her. She did not even know his name. All she knew was that Elsa had a date with a man named Harry and that Harry had a friend in town. Jessi did not even know how Elsa had met Harry. She was clueless about everything, including what to wear.

Thankfully, Elsa was about to arrive to help Jessi get ready for the date. But that did not stop Jessi from pacing the room in her high heels, feeling unsure of herself. Somehow the idea of taking her hot slut act off campus, away from the safety she felt at Thatcher College and into the city itself, with people from the outside, felt like a big step. Logically, she understood why she was going through with it and there was no good reason to turn down a date from someone not affiliated with the college, but that did not settle her any.

"Knock, knock," Elsa called out as she opened the dorm room door. She had visited enough times now to not worry about actually knocking. Jessi and Candi kept an open door policy that meant as long as there was no hair tie on the door handle, anyone could come in, regardless of whether the door was actually open or not.

"Hey, Elsa," Jessi said, smiling. Although her smile looked a little put on, especially with the way that her hands were fidgeting behind her.

"Ooh, I like your hair today," Elsa said. "You've got the wild slut look going. Antwan is gonna love that."

Jessi's smile grew a little wider, a little more genuine, once she heard the man's name that was going to be her date for the night. Antwan. She had no idea what he might look like or what kind of man he was, but now that she had a name to hold onto, she felt much more confident about the whole situation. And as Elsa had said when she first proposed the double date, it was just for the night. Jessi was going to expand her experience with sex and men, all without anything to tie her down.

As for Jessi's hair, she had not finished styling it yet after her shower. She had blown it dry, but had not done more with it, not knowing what the night was going to call for. She did not know how fancy or classy she would need to look. Jessi did not even know where they were going on the date. But those details seemed far less important now that she had a name for the man she would be spending the evening with.

"And I brought you a dress to wear from work," Elsa added. For the first time, Jessi noticed the garment bag Elsa held over her shoulder. Elsa herself was not dressed for a date yet, but she had a habit of arriving early at Jessi's dorm room to change before any evening festivities happened. This was just like those other nights.

Jessi's eyes lit up at that. More and more, Jessi had discovered a joy for shopping. Jessica had not cared for it. Shopping was a chore for her. But Jessi had discovered that she liked finding new ways to show off her body. And with Professor Wright adding to her wardrobe, she now had more clothes than she could hope to wear for any extended period of time. Not that such a fact would stop Jessi from buying more. She had no problems with changing her outfits several times per day. It was actually more fun that way.

It did not take the pair long before they were getting ready for their dates. Elsa had brought sexy dresses for both of them. Jessi's was a yellow halter micro-mini dress with a neckline that nearly went down to her belly-button. She had never worn anything like it, but the moment she donned it, she knew she was in love. The one downside was her belly-button was not actually visible, since that had become a regular part of her style.

Elsa's dress was similar, although since she had bigger breasts, her neckline was not nearly as low. It did feature plenty of cleavage though, with thin straps crisscrossing the opening, making it appear that she was about ready to pop out of the dress at any moment. And it was just as short. Neither woman was going to be wearing any underwear tonight.

Jessi had shoes to match her dress: tall heeled sandals that made her legs look even better. And they made her push out her ass, highlighting the squats she had been performing at the gym. Jessi had a ways to go before she had a bubble butt, but the groundwork was now being laid for an impressive ass.

In all, it took an hour for both women to get ready. Jessi did decide to tame her hair a little bit, but she gave it a slightly windswept look to play up her wildness. By the time Jessi and Elsa left the dorms, they both looked like they were ready for a fun night. They gathered several wolf whistles before they even made it out of the building. Both girls giggled at the responses they collected. It was fun to be wanted like that.

Jessi had offered to drive them, but Elsa insisted on them taking a taxi. That way they were not tied to a car throughout the night. They were completely free to do as they pleased. They could spend the night, split up, or go home early. The evening was completely open to them that way.

The cab driver kept shooting them looks through his rearview mirror, the smile on his face a clear sign that he appreciated the two slutty women sitting in his backseat. Jessi and Elsa spoke in quiet whispers, Jessi trying to pump Elsa for more information about Antwan. Unfortunately, Elsa was not exactly forthcoming with information. She did not know much about Harry's friend. And from what Jessi gathered, Elsa did not actually know that much about Harry either.

Not that such information was needed. Jessi had fucked enough men without knowing their names to know she could not complain about lacking information. As long as Antwan was hot, she was going to be a happy camper. And even if he lacked something in the looks department, that was not necessarily a deal breaker.

"Elsa," came a happy shout as the pair stepped into the restaurant. The taxi had taken them downtown and the restaurant they were being treated to for the date was part of a luxury hotel, but also one of the nicest restaurants in town.

Jessi could only guess that the man calling out Elsa's name was Harry. The moment Jessi saw him, she had to admit that Elsa had good taste, although Harry was a little older than she had figured. She had thought their dates would be in their twenties, but Harry was probably pushing forty. Not that Jessi was in any place to complain. Professor Wright was an older man, although he was still pretty young by professor standards. He was still early in her career as a professor.

But the moment Jessi laid eyes on the man standing beside Harry, her knees almost went weak. If the man was Antwan, she was almost in love just from the sight of him. He was no Cole, who still held Jessi's main interest, but Antwan was a close second. Despite being similarly aged as Harry, Antwan had a strong jaw and a clean-cut appearance that made him look fit enough to play football on the Thatcher College team. If Jessi was not already horny, knowing who her date for the evening was would have gotten her there.

"Hey, baby," Elsa cooed as she ran up to Harry, taking little mincing steps that threatened to cause her short dress to spring up over the swell of her ass. Just before she reached Harry, letting him wrap her up in his arms, she reached back and pulled down on her skirt, needing to maintain her modesty.

As Harry and Elsa kissed, Jessi stalked forward, swaying her hips seductively and licking her pink lips. Antwan turned from looking at Elsa to place all his attention on Jessi. His eyes opened in surprise. It seemed he had not expected such a sexy woman for his date tonight. Jessi might not have had the big tits that other girls had, and she was still adapting to the hot slut life, but she had already developed the ability to be seductive and turn men on. Just the sight of Jessi walking toward him was enough to make Antwan hard.

It was only after Harry and Elsa broke their kiss and embrace that introductions were officially made. Harry introduced Antwan and Elsa introduced Jessi. From all perspectives, Jessi and Antwan made for a good match. They both saw something in the other that they liked. And as Jessi snuck glances at Antwan's crotch, seeing the tent he was pitching as they stood there, she felt confident that he had a cock that would leave her more than a little pleased by the end of the night.

If Jessica had been present in all of this, she would have screamed at the thought of choosing to sleep with a man just because he was hot or because he had a big cock. Especially the last bit. Then again, Jessica had been a virgin and not known the feeling of having a big cock thrust inside of her. Jessi had that experience and knew the kinds of pleasure a big cock could bring her. And it was Jessi who was in charge. And it was Jessi who was licking her lips, imagining what the night could bring her.

It was a short wait for the quartet to be seated at a table. Harry and Antwan made it clear that they were paying for everything, highlighting that fact by ordering one of the most expensive bottles of wine on the menu. No one thought to check either woman's ID. And the waiter did not even blink when both Elsa and Jessi also ordered cocktails for themselves. Sure, they might be a little intoxicated by the end of the night, but they both understood that just enhanced their evenings. Being fun and drunk party girls was a part of the hot slut life.

Interestingly, as the dinner went on, the conversations were a little stilted. This was not because of a lack of chemistry, but more related to where each of the quartet was focused. Jessi hardly said a word to Harry all night. She kept her focus on Antwan, looking at him with a heavily lidded gaze that was meant to entice. When she was not speaking to Antwan, she would briefly giggle and whisper to Elsa. It worked the same way on the other side of the table, with Elsa and Harry mostly talking to each other and with Harry and Antwan sharing occasional conversation.

"I've been in town for business this week," Antwan explained to Jessi. "But I opted to stay in town for the weekend so I can visit with Harry. It's been good to catch up, but I'm leaving early in the morning. You could say this is a going away party for me."

Jessi listened intently, taking in all of that information, already planning how she wanted to celebrate Antwan's last night in town later. She assumed he had a hotel room somewhere, if not here than somewhere nearby. He was certainly dressed well, with a tailored suit, although he had skipped the tie, which only made him look more handsome in Jessi's estimation.

"But what about you?" Antwan asked. "What's your story?"

There was no way that Jessi was going to share that she was a reformed nerd, now choosing the hot slut lifestyle so she could be popular at college. Instead, she explained that she was in college and just trying to enjoy herself.

"Have you selected a major yet?" Antwan asked.

Jessi bit her lip for a moment as she decided how to respond. The truth was, she had not considered that when all of this began. Her desire to be one of the popular girls at Thatcher had left her feeling a bit listless when it came to deciding her future academic life. She needed to choose a major by the end of the school year. Although she still had a lot of time left, the fact she had placed her classes on the back burner seemed to make her decision harder. How could she choose one subject when she was not paying attention to any subject?

"Oh, you know," Jessi tried to answer. "I'm just, like, trying everything still, not wanting to get tied down to something that I don't really like."

Jessi knew she sounded a bit dim like that. She knew she sounded like she was just in college for the parties. That was not true, although given her recent activities and the deal she struck with Professor Wright, she could not exactly say otherwise. The parties and the sex were her major focus now. She had barely opened a book since she returned to school a few weeks ago.

"I get that," Antwan replied. "Besides, you're too pretty to get bogged down with all that hard studying. I definitely see a future for you in other endeavors."

Jessi smiled. With the wine and the cocktails she had slowly consumed throughout dinner, she was past the point where she spotted Antwan's real meaning. She just took it as a compliment that she was hot, which she already knew to be true. After all, she was a hot slut.

Dinner was marvelous and both Jessi and Elsa were clearly having a good time. Harry announced that he wanted to take Elsa dancing and the up and coming hot slut was all for it. Antwan, however, seemed less excited about continuing the evening.

"Jessi, why don't you and I go up to my room for a nightcap?"

There was no way Jessi could turn down such an offer. She readily agreed, knowing exactly where this night was leading.

"See you later, girl," Elsa said. She bounced with excitement, knowing her night was going to go just as well as Jessi's night. "Call me tomorrow sometime. But not too early."

Both girls giggled at that. No, neither of them were going to be up early in the morning. Or, at least, that was Jessi's plan. They hugged and even kissed each other goodbye. Then Harry wrapped his arm around Elsa's shoulder and guided her out of the restaurant, both of them in search of a club that was open on a Sunday night.

"You ready to join me upstairs?" Antwan offered once Harry and Elsa were gone.

"Of course," Jessi answered. She wrapped her arm around

her date's waist. He responded by placing his hand on her ass.

They walked that way out of the restaurant and over to the elevators that would take them up to Antwan's room. And as they walked, Jessi decided she liked having Antwan's hand on her ass. It felt good. Then again, everything felt good in her current state. This was going to be a great night. She was certain of that.

LABELS

"Yes," Jessi moaned as Antwan thrust into her from above. It was their third coupling of the evening and Antwan had demonstrated a stamina that Jessi did not know a man could have. His cock never really went soft. He always seemed ready for more.

First there was the blowjob. Jessi had dropped to her knees as soon as the hotel room door closed behind them and sucked a creamy load from a surprisingly large cock. It had not been long, but Jessi had become a proficient cock-sucker, able to deep throat and everything. However, Antwan's size pushed her to her limits, barely managing to get it past the back of her throat and almost making her gag.

"Fuck," Antwan had groaned with pleasure when his cock finally pushed into Jessi's throat. "Most girls can't get it so deep."

Jessi swelled with pride at those words. She was happy to know that she was not like most other women Antwan had been with. She was a better slut, being able to deep throat his large cock.

And Jessi was rewarded for her hard work, nearly

choking on his dick, because it was not long before her ministrations left him blowing his first load of the night into her mouth. Jessi enjoyed every moment as his seed flowed across her tongue, the flavors lighting up her senses. It was almost as good as the meal that they had just shared. Almost.

The blowjob was followed by a drink from the minibar. Jessi did not particularly care what Antwan offered as long as there was alcohol in it. Jessi was not drunk and she had no intention of drinking too much. This was a night she wanted to remember.

That drink led to a heavy make out session with Antwan holding Jessi's body up against the large windows that over-looked the city below. She enjoyed the way his hands expertly traveled across her body as their lips met, their tongues dancing in each other's mouths. Jessi could feel his hard cock pressing against her and she wanted nothing more than to feel it inside of her. But for now, she let Antwan run the show. He seemed to have a pretty good idea of what he wanted from her. He was her guide and Jessi was perfectly content with that arrangement.

Jessi's mind felt like it was melting as she lost herself in the moment. She was completely aware of the way Antwan's lips felt against her own. And when he started kissing her across her jaw and down her neck to her collarbone, she was about ready to dry hump him right there, wanting or even needing to feel his cock inside of her.

However, while Jessi was focused on the way Antwan's lips traveled across her body, laying down fire against her exposed skin, she completely missed the way he was slowly disrobing her, removing her dress and leaving her only wearing her heels. Even the coldness of the window glass did not clue her into the fact that she was suddenly very naked.

But all that became clear to her when Antwan suddenly turned her around, pressing the front of her body against the glass. His cock was out a moment later and pushing into her from behind. Jessi arched her back automatically, making the angle both better for him and more pleasurable for her. And as he fully entered her, Jessi let out a long, low moan, her body reveling in finally getting filled by the hard cock that had teased her from the moment she had entered the room.

Jessi was not even fully aware that she had been placed on display. With the lights on in the room, anyone on the street below or in neighboring buildings would be able to see her. That was assuming they thought to look. Her naked body was on complete display, but she was completely enraptured by the cock thrusting in and out of her pussy, Antwan's pace growing faster and more erratic as he fucked her harder and harder.

It took everything she had for Jessi to keep from cumming before Antwan did. She bit her lip as she pressed the side of her face against the window. And somehow she managed to hold herself back until she felt Antwan twitch inside of her. It was his point of no return. She started screaming out as the pleasure built inside of her, the dam breaking that kept back all of the evening's erotic energy. It let loose all at once and left her as little more than a rag doll in Antwan's arms.

And all the while he kept fucking her until he spilled his hot cum into her pussy, flooding her with his second load of the night. Jessi's orgasm lasted through the whole thing, her body practically convulsing in his hands. And despite the powerlessness that Jessi felt, she loved every moment. It was hard and fast, but the sensations were more than she had ever imagined. Why bother with sensual love making when she could get fucked hard and fast instead.

It was only afterward, when Jessi started to come down from her orgasmic high, that she realized how much her body had been on display. Anyone could have seen her. And as much as there was a bit of embarrassment that she felt, that was easily overwhelmed by the boost to her arousal, knowing that people could have watched her get fucked from behind. She never knew she had an exhibitionist streak in her, but, then again, it made sense considering her new preferred style that placed her body on display in skimpy clothes and high heels.

After the latest coupling, Jessi and Antwan took another break for a drink. Jessi did not bother to put clothes back on. She simply sat in one of the offered chairs and slowly sipped the latest drink Antwan made for her. It was bright and fruity, whatever it was, and it easily flowed across her tongue and down her throat, the alcohol barely burning on the way down. She was getting better at not just the sex part of being a hot slut, but on the drinking part too.

Jessi had been all set to have an actual conversation with Antwan, but she quickly realized that he just wanted to talk about his work. And that was perfectly fine by her. She actually enjoyed not having to really participate in the conversation beyond nodding her head and letting out the occasional giggle when Antwan told an obvious joke. It meant Jessi could relish the aftershocks of her last orgasm and let herself get turned on all over again, ready for yet another round.

And that was what eventually led to Jessi laying back in the bed with Antwan on top of her. The position reminded her of her first time, but this was so much better. Antwan was bigger, his cock filling her and even stretching her a bit. The pleasure was better too, but this was far less gentle than it had been with Jonas. It was like that first time and the previous moment with Antwan fucking her from behind, pressed up against the window, had been combined into a single moment.

Jessi ran her long nails across Antwan's back. Her hold on

him was not enough to draw blood, but her nails still left red lines across his back.

"Come on, baby," Jessi cooed. "Fuck me harder."

Antwan was already nailing her hard, but his pace and effort picked up at her urging. Jessi had never fully realized that she preferred sex to be hard and rough, not unlike what she saw in those porn videos she watched more and more frequently in her free time. Those videos might not have been real, but they helped to direct her actions when she had a cock inside of her like she did now.

Her partner might have had impressive stamina, but even he had his limits. Jessi did not need to hold back this time either. The moment his cock started to surge with cum, she was cumming too, her body writhing beneath him as her body convulsed with pleasure. It felt like getting hit by a train made entirely of endorphins. Jessi's body lit up and her brain nearly overloaded under the onslaught of pure erotic energy cascading through her in wave after wave, washing over her and leaving her almost drowning in pleasure.

"Fuck," Jessi moaned as Antwan rolled off of her and lay beside her.

"Fuck," Antwan agreed. He had finally met his match when it came to stamina and he was not complaining in the least.

And once it became clear that Antwan was tapped out, Jessi snuggled in next to him and let herself drift off to sleep. There was a smile on her face. It had been a great day with lots of orgasms and other fun sexual activities. Even if Jessi had wanted to go back to being Jessica, there was no way she could give up on the sexy clothes and all the orgasms. She was hooked and there was no turning back. Or so she assumed.

When Jessi woke up, it was still dark outside, but the bedside lamp was on and Antwan was making loud noises from across the room. She raised her head to find him quickly packing a suitcase.

"What's going on, babe?" Jessi asked, her mind still slow to respond after just waking up.

"I've got a plane to catch," Antwan said gruffly. "There's money on the table for you. You never mentioned your price, so I'm leaving what I think you're worth."

"Money?" Jessi asked. She had not expected this. Why was Antwan leaving her money? It did not make sense to her.

"Fuck, you're a dumb bitch," Antwan muttered. "It's just like me to end up with the stupid whores. The whole college thing is probably just a front."

Despite the fact that Antwan was mostly talking to himself, Jessi heard every word loud and clear. He had called her a whore.

"I'm not a whore," Jessi complained.

"Fine, you want to call yourself a prostitute or something?" Antwan countered.

"No, I'm just a slut," Jessi tried to argue, but it was clear that Antwan was no longer listening to her. He walked away from her and entered the bathroom to gather up his shaving kit.

Jessi sat up and pulled her knees to her chest. The blankets fell away from her body, but she did not move to cover herself. She was in shock. Antwan's words kept running through her mind. She had not expected him to fall in love with her. This was just a fun night spent together. That was all. But that did not make her a whore, did it? Jessi felt confused.

Her eyes flitted over to the desk in the corner and she saw the stack of bills there. She had no idea how much money it was. There was no way she had the wherewithal to get up and look. But the money was there. And if she took it, did that make her a whore?

Jessi's mind kept going in circles, trying to argue with itself that she was not a prostitute, that she did not sleep with men for money. But then she saw the cash sitting there and a part of her wanted to take it. She could imagine the outfits she could buy with it. The idea of starting a boob job fund even entered her mind. However, her thoughts kept circling back to whether or not she really was a whore.

Jessi knew she was a slut. That was plainly obvious given her recent actions, but she was pretty sure she was not a whore. That was a level that she had not reached. It was on the other side of a line she did not want to cross.

Antwan returned to the bedroom and finished packing his suitcase. He was already dressed, wearing a slightly more casual, but still good looking, outfit compared to the night before. He looked like a businessman about to get on a plane.

"You can stay until checkout if you want," Antwan said with a shrug. "I don't really care. The hotel will kick you out eventually. You were a hot fuck, but you're nothing more than a whore to me."

With that said, Antwan walked out of the hotel room, pulling his suitcase behind him.

Still sitting in the bed, tears began to flow from Jessi's eyes. Then she started to sob, no longer able to fight back against the hurt she had just experienced. It was not that she denied sleeping with a man she had only just met, but it was the assumption in his eyes that she was a whore, only in it for the money. How had he gotten that impression from her?

But it was more than just Antwan thinking she was a whore. That was just one man's opinion of her. It was an opinion that did not matter, because she never had to see him again. But the question lingered in Jessi's mind. Was she a whore? Was that who she was now? Had she gone too far and passed over the line, taking her from slut to prostitute?

Jessi had no idea how long she sat there, crying. Time

held little remaining meaning as she tried to process what had happened. By the time her sobs finally started to dissipate, the skies were starting to lighten outside. It was still before dawn, but the sunrise was fast approaching.

When Jessi picked up her dress to put it back on for the trip home, she nearly choked when she realized how slutty it was.

"No wonder he thought I was a whore," she said as she slipped it on. It had seemed completely reasonable when she put it on yesterday, but Jessi could no longer accept that her behavior over the past two weeks had been even remotely acceptable.

Jessi did not bother to fix her hair or makeup before she walked out of the hotel room. For the first time, she felt ashamed for her actions the night before. This was a real walk of shame. And it was even more shameful when Jessi realized she had picked up the wad of money left behind by Antwan, slipping it into her purse, before she arranged for a car to take her back to campus.

And it was clear to Jessi that something was going to have to change. She could not keep living like this. Jessi felt nothing but turmoil inside. As much fun as the past two weeks had been, Jessi sensed that she had gone too far. Maybe the life of a hot slut was not actually for her. It was all she could think about as she traveled back to campus. An oversized sweatshirt and baggy jeans had never seemed so attractive before. Nor had doing her homework. Jessica was making a comeback.

MORE FAKE IT UNTIL YOU MAKE IT

If you enjoyed this third season of Fake It Until You Make It, be sure to check out the continuing saga of Jessi as she transforms herself into a bimbo as she navigates college life trying to be a popular girl. The latest episodes (chapters) are available every Tuesday Friday on the Kindle Vella platform. Updates about the story can be found on Tumblr (https://authorsadiethatcher.tumblr.com/tagged/story) Each season of the story will eventually be published in ebook and paperback formats when ready.

ABOUT THE AUTHOR

Sadie Thatcher is a longtime author of erotic fiction, especially related to transformations and bimbofication. She likes to say "I have thrown off the shackles of my conservative upbringing and now write erotic stories."

She maintains a special blog devoted to her writings, including a behind the scenes look at her writing process, and bimbos in general, as well as highlights works by other authors. They can be found at:

https://authorsadiethatcher.tumblr.com

 twitter.com/Sadie_Thatcher

Bimbo Dome

Acting the Part

Subliminal Society

Inheritance

Company Morale

His Bimbo Girlfriend

The Bimbo Room

The Bimbos of Blossom

Dr. Jekyll and Missy Hyde

Second Chance

From M&As To T&A

Trading Places

The Bimbo Nutcracker Suite

Milked and Herded

Fitting In

Clowning Around

Transformative Ink

Choices

Rival Competition

Alien Womanhood

Invasion

The Princess and the Bimbo

Bimbo Labyrinth

The Legend of the Werebimbo

Power and Corruption

The Simulation

The Curse of Playing Bimbo Tag

The Curse of Playing Bimbo Tag: Jenna or Jenni

Simple and Fun Volume 3

Simple and Fun Volume 4

Simple and Fun Volume 5

Simple and Fun Volume 6

Silly Bimbo Volume 1

Silly Bimbo Volume 2

Bimbo Halloween

Bimbo Christmas

Bimbo Technology

Dorm Room Bimbo

Carissa's Magic Pen

Spirit Walk

Muscle Memory

The Case of the Bimbo Wife

Changes

Changes 2

New Year New You

The Bimbo Dream

The Wedding Gift

The Cure

Backfire

Bim & Bo Yoga

Wishing for Each Other

Bimbo Roots

A Bimbo at Oktoberfest

The Lost Bet

The Fountain

Bimbo Ghost

Sugar and Spice and Everything Nice

Basic Bimbo

A Helping Hand

Bimbos in Space

Christmas Train to Bimboton

Letters to Bimbo Claus

Gone Fishing

The Bimbo Behind the Mask

Rival Wishes

What's in a Name?

Playing the Game

Friendly Wishes

My Chemical Bimbo

To Be Young Again

Something Bimbo Calls Him Home

Wishing for Him

The Author Gets Bimbofied

Bigfoot and the Bimbo

Bimbo Zero

Going Native

Thanks for Giving

Working for Bimbo Claus

The Spirit of Bimbo Christmas

The Bimbo Sweater

What Really Happened to D.B. Cooper

Starting Over

Milk and Bliss

The Fighter

The Help

The Bimbo Resort

Awakening

Body Swap Rings: Happy Anniversary

Body Swap Rings 2: Wedding Night

The Bimbo Experience

The Bimbo Experience 2

The Bimbo Experience 3some

The 4th Bimbo Experience

Bimbo Genes

Bimbo Genes II: The Virus

The Bimbo Genes III: The Epidemic

Bimbo Juice: Blue Raspberry

Bimbo Juice: Grape

Bimbo Juice: Mango

Bimbo Juice: Pineapple

Bimbo Juice: Red Apple

Bimbo Juice: Veggie

Bimbo Juice Gone Wild: The Muse

Bimbo Juice Gone Wild: Street Racer

Bimbo Juice Gone Wild: Score

Bimbos of the Traveling Earrings: Book 1

Bimbos of the Traveling Earrings: Book 2

Bimbos of the Traveling Earrings: Book 3

Bimbos of the Traveling Earrings: Book 4

Bimbo Party: Kennedy

Bimbo Party: Esme

Bimbo Party: Ariana

Bimbo Party: Tara

Workout Buddies

Wishful Thinking

Wanting More

Bimbo Harem: Annabelle

Bimbo Harem: Josie

Bimbo Harem: Nikki

Bimbo Harem: Tiana

Giggle Dust

Giggle Dust 2.0

Giggle Dust 3.0

Giggle Dust 4.0

Bimbo Takeover: The First Step

Bimbo Takeover: Teammates

Bimbo Takeover: Going to the Top

Bimbo Takeover: Revenge of the Bimbos

Thanks for the Mammaries

A New Beginning

Copying Kat

Spreading the Love

Discovering Eden

Building Eden

Spring In Eden

Saving Eden

The Perfect Girlfriend

The Perfect Engagement

The Perfect Wife

The Perfect Woman

Be Hot, Not Smart

No Thoughts for Thots

Be Art, Not Smart

The Cream of the Crop

A New Kind of Passion

Getting the Sugar

A Second Lease on Life

Summer

Autumn

Winter

Spring

Edge for Me

Edge Together

Edge and Deny

The Boutique

Lawyer or Beach Bunny

Choosing Sides

Accidental Mayhem

Controlled Mayhem

Planned Mayhem

Jealousy

Desire

Fame

Lessons in the Lab

Nurse Bimbo

Brain Drain

A New Self

Giving In

Corrupted

Bimbo No. 5

Scent of Bimbo

Forbidden Obsession

Goddess Within

The Message

Bimbo Queen

Bachelorette

Beneath the Gown

Honeymoon Surprise

New Rules

Embrace It

Not So Smart

Best of Friends

Joining Bimbodom

Bimbo Salon

Bimbo Vision

Spiral

Rerun